GARGANETTE

To George Frankl

GARGANETTE

The Amazing Story
of a Giant Female

Written & Illustrated
by

SABA MILTON

Ⓖⓟ

OPEN GATE PRESS
LONDON

First published in 1991 by Open Gate Press
51 Achilles Road, London NW6 1DZ

British Library Cataloguing in Publication Data
Milton, Saba
    Garganette.
    I. Title
    823.914 [F]

ISBN 1-871871-09-3

Printed in Great Britain by
Halstan & Co. Ltd., Amersham, Bucks.

Table of Contents

Illustrations

* * * * *

TRANSLATOR'S NOTE

It was while travelling in the region of France around Nantes that this extraordinary manuscript came into my hands. My companion and I had strayed from the familiar and beaten track and found ourselves in uncharted territory, when our vehicle unaccountably stalled and refused to restart. We were stranded late at night in what was to us unfamiliar, and seemed to be unfriendly territory; imagine then our joy on finding, not 3 kilometres distant, an ancient chateau of moderate size, where we were invited with great kindness to remain, until such time as a mechanic could be found and induced to attend to our motor. In the event we remained for 2 ½ weeks, for it was 6 days before the arrival of the mechanic, who had been attending agricultural harvesting vehicles, and then we had to await spare parts. Our hostess, however, an elderly and beautiful woman of noble birth, pressed us with such kindness to stay and make ourselves at home, that we felt entirely at our ease.

Thus it was, that during the second week of residence, I, wandering at liberty in the attics of this place, came upon a stout wooden chest of evident and great antiquity and, impelled by a curiosity not entirely consistent with the strictest rules of conduct laid upon a guest, I opened the chest and was intrigued to find a great pile of papers within, which on closer scrutiny, I perceived to be written in the ancient language of the area. I am by great good fortune, intimately familiar with this tongue and was thus able to read the document with no more difficulty than if it had been Latin or Greek. Some, a very few, of the pages from the top of the pile fell to dust when I unhappily sneezed on them, but the rest of the papers I was able to carry to Madame, begging that she would not reprehend the discourtesy I had displayed in the manner of my discovery, but would allow me to read and translate the papers into the modern idiom, so that the greatest number could receive the undoubted benefit to be derived therefrom.

Madame, I could not help noticing, seemed surprised to see the papers and begged me in her turn, not to read them until I had left her, adding that I might then do as I pleased with them. She said they concerned some member of her family or part of ancient family history on which she did not wish to be questioned. She asked me not to name her or her House, for her sons and grandchildren might be embarrassed, and, as her last condition, enjoined me to return the papers to her when I had done with them, all of which I naturally agreed to do. I was curious to know why the colour had risen in Madame's cheeks on sight of the papers, and why her eyes had sparkled with an exceptional brilliancy, but though I questioned her delicately, she refused to discuss the matter further, and kept the papers by her, giving them up to me only when my companion and I were ready to depart.

I have studied closely the documents so graciously confided to my care, and I have tried faithfully to translate them into accessible modern language, sticking I hope, to the spirit of the original, even when, as so often happens with 'dead' languages, there is no modern equivalent into which a word or phrase may be translated. There is much in the original which may give offence to the delicate modern sensibility: there is some discussion on matters of the body and its functions, for instance, and on violence, which many readers might find startling, but I considered it to be my duty, after great and careful thought, not to censor anything that was, at the time of writing, considered by the author to be relevant to his narrative; and I have not flinched in carrying out my task to the very best of my ability.

Finally, I must add a note in the hopes that the great Lady who first allowed me to take the papers from her will see the completed work and understand. It is unfortunate that I am not able to fulfill my pledge to Madame in all respects: at her request I have not, and will not, divulge her identity, but I cannot return the documents to her, for I have not been able to trace either her or her chateau since leaving it. My companion and I are both notoriously bad navigators and, in my haste to leave the chateau that I might study the papers, I neglected to make a note of its location and even the family name has slipped our memory. But perhaps more serious than this is the fact that the original papers have themselves disappeared, and it is with some shame that I am forced to admit that I left them either on a number 29 bus or at Victoria underground station, on the West bound platform of the Circle Line. All my efforts to trace Madame, her Chateau and the papers have come to nothing. I therefore end with the plea that, if anyone knows of the whereabouts of any of the above mentioned, they will please get in touch with me, care of my publishers, and a generous reward will be given to any person or persons who can give me any information which will lead to the recovery of the original papers.

Sir A Fable

INTRODUCTION

*.......and so large a one had never been seen before. But enough of that: let us return to our muttons. This is the story of Garganette, the true history as told me by my mother who had it from her uncle, who was the third uncle her mother had presented her with, and the kindest and most honourable of men he was too, so you may believe me that not one word of a lie ever passed his lips for a second, it would have died before it was properly born, the atmosphere about him being so pure and holy that nothing so base and worthless as a falsehood ever could stand a chance with him. Take it from me: I met him once when he was a very old man and a sweet odour hung about him even then, which my mother said was the odour of sanctity, though oddly enough, whenever I smell gin I think of this old man, but that is probably an aberration on my part and a coincidence, and is anyway beside the point and definitely not to do with our muttons, which as I said before is all about Garganette.

Ah, Garganette! Now she was the greatest, sweetest, fattest, tallest, most charming and delightful little giant ever to cross the threshold into life, which she did one fine winter day in mid-July, as I recall, and she came into the world not yelling and bawling as other children do, making a nuisance of themselves, but in the most exemplary manner, and the manner of it was - but you shall read later of the manner of Garganette's birth, and her life as she lived it and what she found and how she found it; in fact, everything will be told you just as it happened in life to her, as my mother told it to me in those long winter months when there was nothing better to do than to listen to the story of Garganette. And, really, I don't think there's ever been a better pastime at any time, when alone with one's mother, than to hear

---

The reader will remember that the first few pages being inadvertently destroyed, the translation starts here in mid sentence. AF

4

of Garganette and her doings. And perhaps the best thing about it, is that it is true, every word of it, as I mentioned before, coming, as it did, from my mother's third new uncle and he had it from the horse's mouth, as it were, and the horse had it from Garganette herself. I never met the horse, though it lived to a great age.

If you don't believe any of this then you must just blame yourself - I offer it to you in all good faith, just as I was told it and why shouldn't it be true? It's not as if I were to spin you some really fantastic fairy tale such as, well, er, um, ah! such as, and speaking off the top of my head, you understand, some such ridiculous story as: "Once upon a time there were several men living inside a mountain somewhere, of their own free will, who spent all their time looking for something so small that they couldn't even see it; something that was itself only a part of something so minute that they couldn't see that either. And it wasn't even anything they'd lost: these men only thought it might be there, had a faith, as you might say, in its existence."

"Oh, come on," you would say at this point, with natural scepticism.

"And," I might go on, "in order to find this invisible thing which they thought might be there, these perfectly sane men, well they weren't locked up in the mountain as deluded persons but were highly respected and well thought of, and were paid vast sums of money by all the other people."

"What?" you cry. "Including me?"

"Yes, including you. So then, these men went around inside their mountain throwing other invisible bits at still more invisible pieces in order to ascertain, if they could, the starting point and first principle of life as we know it. And..."

But why go on? Your lips are curled in cynical disbelief and I wouldn't dream of insulting your credence by even mentioning such silly stuff, except by way of an example, as here.

No, what I bring you in this great little history is as true as maybe, and if you don't believe it then fill your bellies with good food and wine and your hearts with love and try again; but don't come snivelling and whining to me about sense and nonsense and it not being what you thought it was going to be and not being true: the sweet breath of Garganette contains more of truth than tiny invisible bits and pieces of God only knows what being hurled at each other inside a mountain. Or so it seems to me.

Yes, read on, read on. Lap it up like good little children at the breast or bottle and you will feel all the better for it.

The Parents Of Garganette And How One Of Them Was Pregnant

To tell properly the story of Garganette, it is necessary that something is said of her parents, for all people, even the best and greatest, and Garganette was certainly that if nothing else, have or had at least two parents, generally speaking; and Garganette was no exception.

It happened that two people, Paul and Mavis Ettin, husband and wife, were to have by their joint efforts, that is, by the assiduous rubbing together of their bacons, a baby. It wasn't their first, but it was to be their last: Mavis was quite determined about that.

"Never again," she had said as she held her first baby in her arms, gazing at it in astonishment as if she didn't know how it happened to be there, and she went on saying the same thing every time she held a new baby in her arms. Now she was about to do it again, and this time when she said, "Never again", she absolutely meant it.

Now, Mavis was a small woman, not a millimetre over 5' 2", give or take a centimetre, but she grew so excessively stout in this pregnancy, that the doctors and others in the ante-natal clinic said, "Really, Mrs Ettin, it's bad for our health to eat so much. We must control ourselves, mustn't we?" and they put her on a diet. But still she got heavier and heavier, and though she swore tearfully that she stuck religiously to her diet, they refused to believe her, and said that if she didn't care about her own health she should at least consider the baby. But it did no good, and she grew more and more gross, so that they couldn't even tell how heavy she was, she having broken every scales in the county, and they got quite sharp with her and told her not to lie about what she was eating. Which, as it happened she wasn't lying, made her most cross and tetchy, so that she said, "Never again," even before the baby had been 7 months in the womb.

How Garganette Was Born

It was a fine hot summer month, with little happening in the way of snow, hurricane, earthquake or flood, and Mavis was in the hospital for a check-up on the progress of her pregnancy, which by the records was almost over.

"Now, Mrs Ettin, and how are we?" said the doctor.

"Fine, thank you, Doctor," said Mavis. "Ooops!" she added suddenly. "The baby's moving."

"Indeed it is," said the doctor, gazing at her with an expression of stupefied alarm on his face; for the great lump at Mavis's middle area seemed to be wandering blindly about in her body.

"Mrs Ettin," he said, "I think your baby's trying to get out."

"Nonsense," said Mavis."It's not due for another 3 days yet. I've had lots of babies and I know. Never one of them early or late by so much as ½ an hour. Oh dear, I do feel a bit strange though."

And watching the enormous movements going on under Mavis's skin, the doctor began to feel a bit strange too. He saw, while he sat in a kind of fit of confusion, the lump slide down her leg, then return and bump around in her bottom. Then it crawled up her back and all at once a finger poked out of her ear, and the doctor screamed. It should be explained that he was a very young doctor and really nothing like this had ever happened to him before.

"Mrs Ettin! Mrs Ettin!" he cried, pulling himself together and remembering his training, which though it hadn't prepared him for this, at least taught him to be calm and moderate in a crisis. "Lie down! Lie down!" and he pushed poor Mavis onto the examination couch, pulled up her legs and yelled, "Down here, baby! This way, come on!" and other encouragements, and there with a leap and a bound, doing a triple somersault, came the prettiest, shiniest, biggest baby the doctor had ever seen.

A great crowd of people, attracted by the noise, came running to the room, and they were quite amazed by what they saw, for it really was remarkable.

8

"It's a girl!" cried the doctor triumphantly, and there was a roar of spontaneous applause. Many people wondered where the doctor had got this enormous baby, for Mavis was shrunk to so small a size now that she was delivered of her burden, that it became almost impossible to see her.

Garganette's First Reaction To The World

But eventually they found her and put the baby in her arms, whereupon Mavis immediately disappeared again. Everyone was talking and laughing excitedly when the baby, in weak, affecting tones, cried, "Food, food!"

"What?" they said. It wasn't that they hadn't all clearly heard and understood, but that they were, perhaps justifiably, taken aback. They were not used to babies talking to them in this way: such things do not happen in well-regulated hospitals.

"Food!" cried Garganette, louder than before. "I only came out because I thought I might get fed. There's not much to eat in there, you know. Oh dear, I do hope they're not going to starve me," and she began to sigh and weep and yell and thrash about. Now, at the sight of a baby in tears they all knew at once what to do. They ran around and collected whatever was to hand, so that for her first meal Garganette ate:

the student nurse's cheese and pickle sandwiches, in their wrapping;
18 bars of chocolate, ditto;
an octogenarian's birthday cake;
27 beef dinners;
12 lamb vindaloo;
63 portions of rice pudding;
11 arctic rolls
and a packet of cigarettes, which had got somehow included.

She washed it all down with 85 cups of tea and 1½ quarts of milk.

She thanked them most graciously by burping, vomitting, pissing and crapping, then, and only then, when the niceties were performed, she settled down to sleep.

How Garganette Was So Called

In the deep and reverential silence that followed, someone whispered, "Gosh."

Then someone else whispered, "Well, I never."

Suddenly everyone was whispering, and comments like, "She's a colossus, a Hercules," and "My, my, my," floated around on every side.

"What are you going to call her, Mrs Ettin?" whispered the midwife.

"Well," muttered Mavis, from under the bulk of her child, "I don't really know."

"With an appetite like that," whispered Matron authoritatively, "you'd better call her Gargantua."

"Gargantua,Gargantua," the whisper was taken up by them all; everyone tried it, "Gargantua," and it being Matron who'd suggested it, no one liked to ask why it was such a good name or to voice the opinion that maybe Joybelle, or Gloria, or Sandra might be more appropriate. Mavis, for instance, particularly liked the name Sandra, but she just didn't like to say.

"Gargantua it is, then," whispered the staff nurse.

Then all at once the baby opened her blue, blue eyes and said, "Gargantua is a boy's name: you must call me Garganette. Now, if you don't mind, I'm very sleepy after all the hard work and excitement of my first day outside, so I'd be most grateful if you'd leave my mother and me to get some sleep. Thank you so much for all your help," and she suddenly yawned so prodigiously that six people were sucked in on the up-draft and disappeared down her throat, never to be seen again.

That is how Garganette got her name, and don't believe it if anyone tells you different: unless, of course, they can prove by scientific methods that what they have to say in the matter is likely to be truer than what I have told you. It's not pride on my part, you understand, I am perfectly impartial in the matter, merely a recorder, but I do not like to see the truth messed around with, except scientifically, of course.

How Garganette Was As A Baby

It can be said that Garganette was the very model of infant perfection, and did everything that a baby should do: her innate good manners prompting her on all occasions as to what duty and etiquette required. Thus, as already shown by her exemplary behaviour in the hospital, she showed her appreciation of all her mother did for her in abundant offerings, pissing great lakes and shitting such mountainous turds that it was the wonder of the neighbourhood. In addition, she ate everything that was offered to her and only yelled and wailed when she was hungry, thirsty, tired, when the widdle and turds she habitually lay in had grown cold and were no longer fun to wallow in, or when she was hot, cold, bored or lonely or felt otherwise moved to comment on her life.

Sometimes out of pity for her wretchedness at being left alone, Paul and Mavis would have her in bed with them, and it was remarkable that all signs of stress and misery left her the instant she found herself between her parents, surrounded as it were, by their reassuring love and affection.

Garganette adored her mother and spurned all toys and comforters in favour of a cuddle from Mavis. Indeed, her joy at being with Mavis was such that, as a little child, she would clutch her mother to her in a goodnight embrace from which Mavis could not extricate herself, nor was she silly enough to try until her child was completely comatose and snoring.

Ah, the ties of love that bind the Mother to the child; the joys of parenthood.

How The Ettin Family Was Moved

Now, the first time Garganette pissed herself there was a flood which ran through the neighbourhood, causing great delight to all the little children, who floated boats on it, fished and swam in it and splashed about as joyfully as if they had been at the sea side on their holidays, screaming with laughter as they pushed each other in the foaming yellow waves and generally making the best of life as they found it. But all the grown men and women were filled with consternation, and thought it was showing off of the worst kind to fill the area with one's own waters; and these in turn complaining to the local authorities, the distress and fuss knew no bounds. Then each time Garganette shat herself it took 789654123 men from that same local authority to take it away, which caused problems for the men and women who ran the place, for some said that this was a waste of local resources and that the rates would have to go up, and some said that it was a good thing as the unemployment problem was being so effectively dealt with, while others said that it would bring the numbers of unemployed persons on the register and claiming benefit down so far that the government would win another election, which some thought a good thing and others thought a bad thing. And other people thought that something should be done with such a valuable natural resource as was Garganette's shit and that it shouldn't be thrown away but stored and used as and when necessary, or it could be sold as manure or made into natural gas to heat the homes of the poor and elderly; whereat others said, yes, that's all very well, but would you want it in your back yard and what are you going to do about it anyway?

Meanwhile, Garganette thrived and when not sleeping, which she being a model of placidity did a great deal, she ate well and drank well and pissed and shat accordingly, so that the problem, no matter which way you looked at it, nor how often you thought about it, or turned away from it and hoped it would go away, grew larger and more difficult, and strong men wept at the very idea of it, and the problem seemed insurmountable, until one person working in that department charged with finding a solution, got so tired with being constantly harassed by all the people who did nothing, that she decided the best and only thing she could do about it was to pass the buck, and so it was arranged that the Ettin family and their wonderful daughter should be removed to the countryside, where a farm was found for them, that being the best place, it was thought, for such a lot of manure.

So it happened that one fine day, early in the night, in the very spring of autumn, Garganette, in a fine open carriage on the railway train and waving her legs to the passers-by, proudly escorted her family to their new home in the great and glorious countryside, which it was felt would be so much more healthy for her, and where she could grow into a happy and normal child.

Of Garganette's Brothers And Sisters

Be it known that Garganette had six sisters whose names were: Nora, Laura, Cora, Dora, Flora and Michelle; and six brothers who were called: Michael, Nicholas, Richard, Victor, William and Benedick.

Of her sisters Garganette was soon able to distinguish one from the other by noticing that Laura was pretty, Flora was tall, Dora was short, Nora was kind, Michelle sounded different and that Cora was always right. With her brothers she found that Mick was fierce, Nick was strong, Rick was brave, Vick was fat and Willie and Dick were fun.

How Mavis In The Peace Of The Countryside Began To Question Certain Things

Now that the tribulations and normal confusions attendant upon the birth of a child that every Mother feels were behind them, Mavis found it possible to relax somewhat from the cares of city life and the constant threat of what the neighbours might tell each other, which so much occupied her formerly, and, before noticing that the country too had stresses and pressures of its own, though, of course, fewer neighbours, Mavis found that she had some time to address herself to a problem or nagging doubt which had begun to formulate itself at the very time of Garganette's birth, and now forced itself into her consciousness with great vigour and persistence.

"I don't understand it," she said to her husband, Paul.

"Ah, what's that then?" asked her husband, Paul.

"Well, I'm just an ordinary sort of woman, and so are you and well, why does it happen to us?"

"Ah," said Paul. "What's that then?"

"Well, there we were quietly getting on with it and making babies like you're supposed to and just living and all that, and now we have to live in the country, and well, what's wrong with Garganette?"

"Well," said Paul, "I think she's a lovely baby."

"Yes," said Mavis, "but Paul, she's bigger than me already and she's only 4 months old."

"Well," said Paul. "There is that."

But though a problem shared might be a problem halved, Garganette continued to grow at a rate which alarmed Mavis, and Mavis was still unable to understand what it all meant.

The Genealogy Of Garganette

This is the true genealogy of Garganette, which, had Mavis known about it, would have helped her to understand her daughter's wonderful capacity for growth.

The great Pantagruel, whose family tree is given in the famed account of his life, married late in years his half-cousin or second foster child eight times removed, the renowned and terrible Badedin, and she in the fondness of her body gave him 50 daughters, and no matter how insistent Pantagruel was that he must have a son, she refused to give him one, and insisted equally forcefully that he would have daughters, if need be, until he was over-run by them as a granary with mice. Which so it proved.

Now Pantagruel took an enormous delight in these girls of his and would not allow any man to know them more intimately than he himself did, for he would not tolerate the idea, and he kept them close by him except one, and she the youngest of them all, who had wit and deviousness and outlived her father, he leaving them orphaned in his 875th year. This child, named Malnoise by her mother, but later called Lovelybonk or Good-fuck, for the reason that she gave great pleasure by her beauties to as many men as there were shells on the sea shore, gave birth to as many sons and daughters as could be found in any medium sized to large town, among whom were many heroes, but she being unmarried all her sons and daughters were considered at that time of prurience as being beyond redemption and were outcast and called bastard and no one would name them and they became as shy of publicity as deep-sea fish, so that by virtue of the world's censorious neglect, many of this noble family disappeared and took to the hills becoming reclusive and hidden.

It was at the age of only 463 years that the good Lovelybonk passed peacefully away, secure in the knowledge that she had done her best to re-people the earth with her kind and had enjoyed herself up to the limit and hilt of all enjoyment. But times were changing and giants were no longer credited, and, as the world grew colder, her children that were left sought to conform, and crammed themselves into the tiny homes and dwelling places of their neighbours, hoping by means of anonymity to win favour and good repute, so that in less time than it takes to tell, Lovelybonk's children were completely indistinguishable from any other lawyers, shopkeepers, road sweepers, petty crooks and what you will. For generations it continued so, until at last the degenerate and enfeebled strain of giant genes fetched up in the person of Mavis Ettin, and, shrink as she might and cram herself into whatever little space she could, and although she assumed the mask of the ordinary and everywhere passed as normal, she was in fact and without knowing it, one of the last and smallest giants in England.

How Garganette Traced Her Ancestry Beyond The Furthest Reaches Of Time On Her Father's Side

Adom was the first man, born of his mother the Earth and his father the Sun. He was a giant, the first ever seen, and a terrible giant he was too. There was nothing he could not do; for he could cross whole continents at one stride; walk the deepest seas with his feet on the ground, and perform so many wonders that the records of his works fill many a book from the ancient libraries. He built the mountains from his own waste, which is to say shit, and deepened the seas with his own waters, which is to say piss. And truly wonderful he was. And in course of time Adom begat Admo, and Admo begat Doam, and Doam begat Moad, and Moad begat Mishae, and Mishae begat Mashae, and Mashae begat Hephthae, and Hephthae begat Hethphae, and Hethphae begat Phthaehe, and Phthaehe begat Thphahae, and Thphahae begat Loa, who was not tall.

And Loa begat Higha, and Higha begat Zograthorea, and Zograthorea begat Toh, and Toh begat Foh, and Foh begat Ate, and Ate begat Moh, and Moh begat Less, and Less begat Nizcchoeabnizz, and Nizcchoeabnizz begat Nil and the line would have died out but that Nizcchoeabnizz took unto himself in the ninety-third year of his reign an second wife who was young in years and fertile as the plains of Conzomaccha for that she already had twenty sons, and she bare him her what'sit and in due time a son, that was an giant in the land, and the like of him had not been seen in an hundred generations, and his name was called Maximumius, which if we transliterate it from the ancient tongue means the most or greatest, for that he was the most great that had been seen. And Maximumius begat Torius, and Torius fell off his horse in love and begat an son that was called Claudius for that he was lame, and Claudius begat Mozzarella, and Mozzarella begat Gorgonzola, and Gorgonzola begat Feta, and Feta begat Brie, and Brie begat Wenslydale, and Wenslydale begat Cheddar, and Cheddar begat Haloumi, and Haloumi begat Camembert, and Camembert begat Cambazola, that was an bastard, and his brother also that was called Cheeze. And it came to pass that Cheeze murdered Cambazola and all his issue also, for that bastardy was at that time held to be illegimate and the Law did say that none that was an bastard should inherit the land, for so it was written. So that none of this issue of Cambazola survived saving only one, an daughter of his, who in the nineteenth year of her age was as fair as the fairest flower, as tall as the highest mountain and as broad also, and as strong as an thousand warriors, for she was an giantess and the like of her had not been seen in the land for an hundred ages and her name was Emmentale, and Cheeze took Emmentale unto his wife.

And Emmentale was an good and dutiful wife unto her husband, Cheeze, saving only that she did eat her children whensoe'er that she was hungry, but so many sons did she bare that an few more or less would not be missed, and of her sons she did eat they were called Lymeswold, Gruyere and Blue Brie, Monosodium Glutamate and Eenumbers, so that she did burp horribly and tare her hair and beat her breast.

But of her sons which survived the slaughter of his mother's teeth, none was greater than the mighty Nacker, who from out his loins did begat an hundred and twenty sons each of an hugeness that it was astonishing to behold, and the least of these sons was greater than an army in full battle before that it should take to flight.

And Nacker begat Hug, and Hug begat Rug, and Rug begat Drug, that was an man who in the exigency of his hours did see visions, but none could understand an word of what he meant, and Drug begat Smug, and Smug begat Arrogant, and Arrogant begat Pompous, and Pompous could not find unto wife an honourable spouse, for that he was unbearable and would not be able to father an child that could be borne, but that by his trickery and long purse he did get his monstrous fat hands upon an sweet young woman that knew no better, and Pompous knew her and she bare him one son that was called Postumous, for that his father was accidentally done to death by an long knife and sharp enough, which from his mother's hand did slip, before the child was born.

And Postumous begat Arachnaphobe, and Arachnaphobe begat upon his wife an hundred spidery men, that caused their father to gasp and gape, and were by his insistence driven from his kingdom, but one survived and was called by his mother Son.

And Son begat Son, and Son begat Son, and Son begat Son, and Son begat Son, and Son begat Son, and Son begat Son, and Son begat Son, and Son begat Son, and Son begat Son, and Son begat Son, and Son begat Son, and Son begat Son, and Son begat Son, and Son begat Son, and Son begat Son, and Son begat Son, and Son begat Son, and Son begat Son, and Son begat an daughter that was called Amazing, for that she was such an surprise to all about her, that had not seen her like for years without number. And she by the necessity of her desires took unto herself an husband that was greater than all the others there had been, and of him she was brought to bed of an healthy boy, that was the delight of the people for that he ruled wisely and was enlightened in his bearing, by the grace of God, and his name was Eddlebeg, for that he was mighty.

And Eddlebeg begat Ethelben, and Ethelben begat Athelbum, and Athelbum begat Mordlespun, and Mordlespun begat Anzleturd, and Anzleturd took unto wife Coldwomb and they made by their connubations Shoveprick, and Shoveprick begat Muddlefuck, and Muddlefuck begat Paul that was called Ettin, and Paul begat Garganette that was the greatest of all her line since the birth of her many times Great Grand Father Adom.

And so it was that Paul, the only other giant, albeit small, in the land, met and married Mavis and they, without knowing it, were the last giants of their time, and what with one thing and another, given their common great ancestry, their genetic mix, the state of the nation, the constellation of the stars, and whatever it was that Garganette brought with her herself, it was inevitable that one day, if they tried hard enough and for long enough, they would probably definitely have a child of immense proportions whom they would call Garganette.

It is vital to stress here, and it cannot be too forcefully maintained, the importance of knowing as much as possible, if possible everything, about the person with whom one decides to breed: if Paul and Mavis had only checked properly, they would have been aware of the likelihood of one, at least, of their children being, what they came to consider, totally extraordinary. As it is, they carelessly went at it with a blind will like knives, and look what happened to them. Be warned.

How Garganette Continued To Grow

Although Garganette's growth was completely natural and, as you have seen, completely normal given her heritage, Mavis could not see it that way and she watched anxiously to see if she could see how it was that Garganette grew so much, so, as it were, flauntingly, so obviously large. But she couldn't see anything that would give her an idea of how Garganette grew.

"If only I could catch her at it I could put a stop to it," Mavis said to her husband, Paul.

"Oh, yes," said Paul. "What's that then?"

So at last Mavis went to see the doctor, and said, "Please Doctor, could you please give me something for the baby, because you see, she won't stop growing."

And the doctor said, "Well, Mrs Ettin, it's perfectly normal for babies to grow, you know. It's healthy, you see. How much does she weigh?"

"I don't know, Doctor, but she's enormous," said Mavis tearfully.

"Well, well, Mrs Ettin," said the doctor, kindly, "it can't be very serious, you know, if she's growing, not if she's eating properly, and if she's growing I suppose she must be eating properly. But you do seem a bit run down so I'll give you something for your nerves, some nice tranquillisers. Do try them; they're the ones I use myself so they can't do any harm, now can they? Now don't you worry. Thank you. Do come again if you want to have another little chat about, well anything, you know. Good bye. Thank you. Good bye." Some people, thought the doctor to himself when Mavis had gone, do have the strangest fears. Worried about a baby growing, I don't know. Now, he thought, I think I'll have a couple of tranquillisers myself. Mmm, nice.

Mavis went home and took the tranquillisers and watched Garganette most carefully, but still Garganette continued to grow and to be the most perfectly happy baby in the world. Mavis told Paul that he must go to the doctor.

"Doctor," said Paul, "you must give me something for the baby. She is growing rather a lot, though of course I don't mind as there is plenty of room in the country, isn't there, but it worries my wife and she's most upset about it. She says its irregular and not normal, and I think she thinks the baby's doing it on purpose, and she has twelve babies already, and she should know something about it by now, I should think, but I must say, I don't think the baby is doing it on purpose, and as I say, I don't mind, but really it isn't up to me and it's my wife who has to see to it all."

"Ah," said the doctor, "give her these nice pills and don't hesitate to come back if you want to. Thank you, do call again, thank you, good bye."

But the tranquillisers didn't make Garganette stop growing and being the most happy baby anyone had ever seen, and so Mavis and Paul went to see the doctor together and said that he must do something about it. Then the doctor wrote to the Health Visitor, but she refused to go, because, she said, they were a strange family, everyone knew that, and had the most enormous baby of which she, the Health Visitor, speaking personally, was afraid, and in her opinion the doctor ought to go himself.

The doctor, thereupon, wrote a letter to the District Health Authority insisting on immediate help for an outbreak of paranoia brought on by fantasies of big babies, which if it went unchecked would soon assume epidemic proportions; he insisted also that the Health Visitor be suspended from her duties, pending a full inquiry; and finally asked them to send a psychiatrist to attend the Ettin family on their farm, as it was they who seemed to be at the centre of this creeping, insidious problem.

Then he took two tranquillisers in ½ a pint of gin and went on a long weekend.

How Paul Was Carried Away On A Tide
Of His Own Making

One morning Garganette, waking from her honest sleep, was taken with the urgent desire to pass from her body the waste water which had accumulated within her. This she immediately did, and let it loose from her urethra or pee hole.

Now her father Paul saw her and kissed her, saying, "What a wonderful child you are, Garganette, a constant marvel to me," and he went to his work in the fields. And while he worked he thought of his daughter peeing and was suddenly overtaken by a marvellous mass of water, so great that it had burst from her window and fell in a rushing, splashing, sparkling waterfall and when it hit the ground was instantly transformed into a dashing river, the force of which lifted Paul clean off his feet and carried him along with it, which so delighted Garganette that she laughed and clapped her hands and was encouraged to treble her efforts to replenish the seas of the earth, and on and on she went, making water for the good of all; while Paul, caught up in this flood of his daughter's making and carried along willy nilly, cried out to his men who worked in the fields as he passed them to come and get him out, but the current was too strong for them and they fell in with great splashes, one after another and could not get out. And still the river rushed on, for Garganette still peed.

More and more men working in the fields ran to help their neighbours and in they all fell too, until Paul was at the front of a great army of farmers being borne along on the crest of this new river, now twirled one way by eddies and whirlpools and now twiddled another way. So Paul floated on. He began to enjoy himself, once the initial shock had worn off; he began to sit up and take note. A thrill of great delight took hold of him at the very centre of his being, and down there, between his legs, he began to feel very perky and interested.

"Hey, lads!" he cried out to the men following on behind."What do you think of Garganette's river?"

"Ah, she's a fine one, your daughter, and no mistake," they replied.

"Say lads!" then cried Paul, "let us take ship and make sail to strange lands and pastures new. We shall meet many wonderful adventures in many wild lands. We shall perform many great feats of arms among weird foreigners. We shall sail the seven seas and roam the seven continents. Are you with me, lads?"

"Aye, Capt'n!" they cried, as one man with one glad voice.

Their ship was a beauty, with seven great sails, white as a bird's wing, white as the foam on the high wave's crest. Her decks were as broad as a great cricket pitch and her anchor as deep as the mind of a maid. Her aircraft hangar carried seven great planes, and on her stern sprit was the rocket launch pad where her seven man rocket pointed straight to the sky, primed, glistening and ready for flight.

"Ahoy, there, me hearties!" cried Paul from the bridge. "Haul anchor! Belay there! Look lively, me boys! There's work to be done, deeds to perform, treasure to find!"

"Aye, aye, Capt'n, sorr!" they all cried.

Oh, what fun they had: what storms they rode when all heaven was pitted against them; what thirst they endured when, out of fierce blue skies, ne'er a drop of rain fell for weeks and weeks; what shipwreck, hunger, privations and scurvy. How many were lost, empassioned by love of the naughty sirens; how many poor souls, maddened by sorrows, plunged into the watery depths to be lost forever. How many nights under the clear star-decked velvet sky did they spend singing melancholy songs or shanties of the sea, home, love and the fecklessness of women. Tears they wept, nights they slept, fights they brawled until one day -

"Land ahoy!" piped the clear fluting tones of Mid-shipman Sweetheart.

"Pull in the mainsail, foreshorten the topsail, unleash the other! Ahoy there!" cried Paul. "Look lively! Go easy! Drop anchor!

We're there!"

"Hurray!" cried the men, and they all swarmed ashore with Paul at their head.

"I claim this land for Queen Garganette, my daughter!" cried Paul, brandishing his cutlass.

"Hurray!" cried the men, brandishing theirs, "for Queen Garganette." And Paul immediately led them on a search for the wicked dragon, from whom they were to free the beautiful Princess.

"Princess," cried Paul, "we have come, in the name of Queen Garganette to free you from the wicked dragon. Do you wish to be free to serve the Queen, my daughter, Garganette?"

"Oh, sir," sighed the beautiful Princess, "you are brave and bold, but can you beat this vile dragon? Free me but once, and I will serve your daughter, the noble Garganette, for ever."

"Then, Princess," cried Paul, "just let go the dragon's rein and stand aside. Come, you ignoble beast, stand up and fight! You've met your match at last. I, Paul, shall fight you and, by Garganette, I'll win!"

Whereat the dragon roared such a mighty roar that the Princess and all the men fled. Then Paul immediately cut off its head and its blood gushed out hugely.

"Hurray!" cried the men.

"Ah, Princess," cried Paul, "you are free!"

Then the men filled up the hold with gold and diamonds and precious stones and they all set sail for home.

"Great Queen and Daughter Garganette!" cried Paul as he fell on one knee; and he poured precious treasure and gold into her lap and gave her the Princess to play with.

Garganette was so pleased to see him that she laughed, and hugged him and kissed and cuddled him and petted him and licked him and ate him all up, for, of all men, she dearly loved her father, Paul.

How The Results Of The Doctor's Letter Were Most Pleasing To Garganette

One bright sunny day there was a knock on the farmhouse door and in came the nicest, brightest, sunniest, most handsome man that Garganette had ever seen. He was wearing a brown suit and a straw hat. He was totally remarkable because his bright eyes saw, his ears heard, his hands could touch and he was smiling a big smile. He was altogether alive in the most complete way possible.

"How do you do?" said this wonderful and charming man to Mavis when she opened the door. "My name is G. Porgie."

"Oh, yes," said Mavis.

"I'm the psychiatrist from the hospital. I understand that you have a problem I might be able to help you with."

"Oh, Doctor," said Mavis, "thank heavens you've come. It's the baby, you see, she seems to be ill in some way. She won't stop growing."

"Well," said Mr Porgie, "let's have a look at her then. Where is she?"

"In here, Doctor," and Mavis took him into the baby's room.

And there she was: blooming, blossoming, growing big and splendid, and the moment she set eyes on Mr Porgie, Garganette crowed with delight, just like a happy little animal seeing the most delicious thing imaginable.

"Well," said Mr Porgie, charmed by the large amount of beauty that Garganette represented. "Well, I say. Hullo, baby. What seems to be the trouble then?"

At which Garganette answered him by grabbing him in her great fist and with manifestations of tremendous delight, popped him right up inside her.

Oh, what fun she had.

"Oh!" cried Mavis. "Oh, Doctor! Oh, what must you think? Oh, Garganette, give him back at once! Oh, let him out! Oh, Paul, oh help, oh Doctor, ohohoh! Oh, whatever will the neighbours say?! Oh, help! Oh, dear! Oh, oh, oh, oh, oh!" and she flapped her hands at Garganette, and ran around crying like a strange straggly chicken, making odd noises, but nothing she could do would make Garganette give Mr Porgie back.

But at last, when Mr Porgie finally came out, he seemed, though dazed and glazed, to be the happiest man in the world. He leaned against the great bulk of Garganette's leg with a beatific smile on his face.

"Mrs Ettin," he said, when he had got his breath back, "I can tell you there is absolutely nothing wrong with your daughter. Not at all. She is a truly wonderful and remarkably clever child."

Garganette gave him a great, big sloppy kiss, and he went away at length, promising to come back at the earliest opportunity.

"Well," said Mavis. "Well, I never did. What a funny man."

But notwithstanding what Mavis might say, Garganette thought he was a marvellous man, and she and he were always the very best of friends.

How Garganette Grew Her Teeth

Garganette felt in her gums an excitement which caused her to become most lively, and in seeking to gratify the desire which underlay this sensation, she put into her mouth everything that came to hand: stones and rocks were crumbled between her gums; buildings were shattered; the church steeple became as dust. She gummed to death a whole herd of elephants, and six woolly rhinoceri, the last of their kind on earth, suffered the same fate, but she found the animals quickly became soggy and distasteful, and she spat them out. Conservationists all over the world were, naturally, up in arms, and there was an outcry, but what could they do? What can you do when a child is growing her teeth?

She then moved to the forest and tore up all the trees in an attempt to find a comforter for her sprouting gums, but the trees she chewed instantly became matchsticks, and a huge match boxing factory had to be set up to deal with the immense stocks she had produced. All match making had to cease worldwide until the Garganette Brand was used up, which, with the anti-smoking lobby and the decline in the Boy Scout movement, was a lot longer than might have been expected. But none of this activity was in any way helpful to Garganette in her search to satisfy the longing in her mouth.

Garganette did not despair however, being constitutionally incapable of such a state of mind, and eventually her admirable persistence and staying power were rewarded when, looking around for something that would answer her needs, she saw a man. Such a good looking, chunky, chubby, love of a little man he was, that she grabbed him up, cooing sweetly, and put him straight to the test. Her eyes had not deceived her, and from the first nibble she knew she had found what her clamorous gums desired. She developed quite a taste for men, and whenever the need arose, she would reach out for the nearest, whoever he happened to be, and she sucked and munched and crunched her way through an army of delicious men, so that if there had been a king in need of soldiers to fight his wars, he would have been very disappointed and puzzled to find only a few scrofulous and disgusting old scallywags, whom Garganette never touched on a point of principle, finding the clean and wholesome much more toothsome and far better suited to her. But there was no king, only a Queen, and she of a peaceable nature, so Garganette was left to get on with it to her gums' desire. Mind you, there was some complaint from among the women, who found their men disappearing, but that's just like men, isn't it, to slope off at the first opportunity? You can't trust a man, can you?

So it was that with the aid of all these wonderful, kind men, Garganette was soon the proud owner of one very fine tooth, as bright as a full moon, as white as pure cow's milk, and as strong, well, you can take it from me that there never was anything as strong as Garganette's teeth, which became a by-word for all that is strong and wonderful.

Now that she had successfully grown her first tooth she wanted to show off its wonderful properties to her family, and proudly bit off the head of her sister, Michelle, and would have eaten the whole of this child, had not Paul and Mavis persuaded her to give up the idea.

Mavis had many anxious moments putting Michelle back together again, but the love a Mother feels, even for the least of her children, triumphed, and Michelle, who no longer limps, tells the story of how she once visited the gullet of her wondrous sibling, and survives to dine out on the occasion right up to the present time.

How Garganette Played The Shitting Game

Garganette had fine bowels. That this is true and no lie can be seen from the immense capacity for shitting she showed even from birth. My goodness, she loved to shit, to crap, turdulate and besmirch her bottom with the fine smelling ordure from the plentiful store in her bowels. In at the mouth went the food and just in its own good time, after its journey round and round the intestines great and small, it came out, lickety spit, ploop, plop, poop. Masses of it. Truly.

Ah, the lovely feel of warm golden turds as they ambled their way from bowel to anus, down the passage, and Ah, yes, there it comes, a great, fat, long, soft, firm, beauteous snake of smelly, lovely, squidgey, sweet, glorious shit. Mountains of it. Could you believe the quantities the dear child was capable of, and indeed, was in the perfectly regular habit of producing from her arse, if I didn't tell you and you didn't trust me implicitly to tell you the truth?

If you could have seen the expression of eager anticipation on her sweet face and the joyous passion she palpably evinced on

successful completion of her primary duties. Ah, what a ᵖ
vision, to see a good child so well occupied as to be frɛ.
gladly, lightheartedly shitting and then, with the dedication oɩ
the true artist, inspecting the results.

So great was her love of the turd, that she made a study of the
subject, going into the matter in such depth that, before her third
year amongst us, she was the foremost expert in all the land, and
the monograph she published at this time, her first work of any
note, proves beyond doubt that she knew her stuff.

How Garganette Grew Even Larger And Did Other Things Which Caused Her Mother Deep Concern

Now, Garganette was the biggest little girl ever recorded since
records began, and Mavis, her mother, was filled with confusion
by this, for of all things Mavis preferred, when possible, to be
normal and to be seen to be so, but after much thought Mavis
devised a plan which she felt sure would lead to a resolution of
the problem, and in accordance with this plan she detailed her
other children to watch their baby sister and to tell at once if and
when they saw her growing.

Norah and Laura, Dora, Michelle, Vick, Mick, Flora and Nick,
Rick, Willie and Dick all played with Garganette and watched
her with care in the bedroom, the sitting room, the shitting room,
the shower room, the bathroom, the lounge, the spare room, the
reception room, the long room, the drawing room, the box room,
the gallery and the L-shaped room. They played with her in the
meadow, the barn, by the river, round the pond, in the lake, on
the hill, in the valley, through the forest, in the copse, wood and
spinney; in the long grass, the short grass, among the meadow
sweet, willow herb, rag wort, lady's slipper, buttercups, daisies,
dandelion, pimpernel, forget-me-not, snow drop, crocus, blue-
bell, primrose, violet, daffodil, orchid and bryony, larkspur,
marguerite, marigold and foxglove; they wouldn't let her eat the

deadly nightshade, any toadstools or the poison ivy, though she sincerely wanted to; they kept her out of the granary and the slurry, the pig-pen, the sheep fold, the sheep dip, the cow shed, their father's way and harm's way; off the high road, the low road, the long road, the straight and narrow, the slippery slope, the motorway, the high way and the by-way; they valiantly saved her from falling in the river, in case she should bump her head on the bottom or cause a flood, and while she slept they played hide-and-seek and chase all around her. But they never saw her growing, and all Mavis ever heard were shrieks of laughter interspersed with mysterious silences. And still Garganette grew bigger and fatter and more round and cheerful than ever.

Then one day Cora came running to Mavis.

"Mum, mum! Come quick!" she cried. "She's definitely growing, I seen her, and she's playing with her Thingy!"

"WHAT?" cried Mavis. "WHAT!! PLAYING WITH HER THINGY?! OH! OH! OH! NO! NO! NO! AFTER ALL I'VE DONE FOR HER! WHAT!! PLAYING WITH HER THINGY?! Oh, oh, my poor heart! WHATEVER WILL BECOME OF US ALL? WHAT HAVE I DONE TO DESERVE THIS? OH OH OH! YOU ALL TREAT ME SO BADLY! WHAT SHALL I DO? WHATEVER WILL THE NEIGHBOURS SAY!!!!! AARGH! AAARGH!" went Mavis and she rushed to Garganette.

"AAARGH! AAARGH!!" cried Mavis, when she found her baby playing in the sunshine. "AAARGH!!! You bad girl! Playing with your Thingy!!!! And in the open too!!! AAARGH!!!! WHATEVER WILL THE NEIGHBOURS SAY?!!!!!! WHAT WILL THEY THINK?!!!!! AAAAAARGH!!!!!!!!!!!!!!" and she ran round in circles with her hair all flying, and Garganette thought it the funniest thing she had ever seen.

"HA HA HA!" laughed Garganette.

"AAAARGH!! AAAARGH!!! AAAAARGH!!!!" cried Mavis, spinning round and round like a top.

"OHO HO HO!!!!" laughed Garganette, holding her hands to

her sides to keep from falling over.

"AAAARGH!!! AAAARGH!!!!" cried Mavis, and she lay down and kicked the ground with her heels, then she turned round and beat the grass with her fists, bit great chunks of it, spat it all out, then sat up and screamed again. Then she stopped.

"He he he," laughed Garganette, "funny little mummy. Do it again, mummy, please do it again!" and she clapped her hands and laughed again. Then she picked Mavis up, gave her a great, big, huge wet kiss, and jiggled her up and down on her knee.

And after that, though it is strange to relate, and though Garganette still kept right on getting bigger and bigger, nothing was ever said on the subject again.

How The Children Played On The Farm

Garganette, Willie and Dick played the following games with the bull: first Willie and Dick rode on the bull's back and the bull stamped and roared and threw them off, this was called Pitch and Toss. Then Garganette chased the bull twice round the field one way, after the bull chased her twice round the field the other way, so that they shouldn't get giddy; then Garganette leapt over the bull as the boys crept under him, which was Leap Bull Creep Bull; then they played Bull in the Middle, when the three children ran around the bull laughing and shouting while the bull, pawing the ground and snorting, decided which one to charge first; then they played Tag, and the bull was It. Then Blind Bull's Bluff, Hide and Seek, Hunt the Pizzle, Ring-a-Bull-a-Roses, Postman's Knock, Sardines, Marbles, Five Stones, Jacks, Skipping, at which the bull excelled, Musical Chairs, I Spy With My Little Eye, which the bull won, True, Dare, Kiss or Promise, Follow My Leader and O'Grady Says.

Then they played Cowboys and Indians, Mothers and Fathers, Doctors and Nurses, Surgeons and Patients, Cops and Robbers, Monks and Nuns, Angels and Devils, Americans and Russians,

Catholics and Protestants, Pirates, Shipwrecks, Treasure Hunters, Astronauts, and the bull was so good at all these games and so clever, that he became King of the Castle, Bull of the Walk, the Bull in the Moon, the Papal Bull and the President of the United States. Then he suddenly remembered his duties and responsibilities and rushed off to take up the sacred Office entrusted to him by a free and noble people, and he did it very well, because, as he said when he came back, they spoke his language there. Then they all four fell into a heap for a rest, and lay in most pleasing concord, one leaning on the other, and they breathed in each other's ears, gazed up each other's noses to pull out the worms they found there, picked each other's teeth, peered into each other's eyes and listened to each other's hearts until it was time for tea.

How Garganette Helped On The Farm

Garganette's life on the farm was a happy one and she helped her father, Paul, in as many ways as she could find. The first thing she did each morning was to water all the fields from the plentiful supply in her own body. Then she milked the cows, all of them by mouth, before Paul was even awake, and led them out of the brand new, automatic milking parlour and into the bull's field so that they shouldn't be lonely. She herded the pigs into the orchard, where she helped them harvest the fruit with her own teeth until her stomach was completely full and could hold no more, whereupon she laid a rich manure on the burgeoning wheat. She let the hens out of the factory and the rats into the granary; she put the sheep among the lettuces, taught the cats to swim and the dogs to climb trees. She busted the dams to let the trout slip away to pastures new; scattered seed on stony ground; put the cat among the pigeons; the nigger in the wood pile; spokes in all the wheels and enough spanners in the works to bring down an empire. She even found, after much riotous searching, the needle lost by Mavis in the hay stack.

Then she took all the eggs she could lay her hands on and all the mushrooms and got Mavis to make her an omelette for breakfast.

How Paul Made A Decision

It happened, through no fault of his own except that he had so little experience in these matters, that Paul soon found himself facing ruin. He worked very hard but he could not prosper. Every time Garganette let the hens out of the factory, he had to buy new ones for her to let out; every time he loaded the baby calves into the cattle truck to take them to market, Garganette let them out again and put them back with the cows. Each time she put the weaners back with the sow and he took them away again, she returned them to their mother.

When he had the fields sprayed with weed killer, the smell made her sneeze so much that the plane was blown off course and the pilot made a trip round the world, quite unscheduled and, this happening on his wedding day, put all his plans out of sync and made him so cross that he refused to come back and fly over Paul's fields again. Garganette loved the pilot and was sorry that he wouldn't be coming back again. She loved everyone and everything. She loved the animals; she made a daisy chain of sheep because she loved to feel their fleecy bodies against her skin and hear their soft bleating in her ears; the lambs frolicked in her hair; the pigs played jumping games over her toes and the bull rubbed his horns against her ankles. They were all, from the hens pecking in the hedgerows, to the cows grazing in the corn, delightfully happy, Garganette perhaps most of all, and Paul, like the good father he was, took his daughter's advice to become an organic farmer and so eventually made an immense fortune.

How Garganette Was Prepared For School

It was time that Garganette must go to school and it became necessary to equip her properly with a uniform in brown and yellow, for these were her school colours, and neither she nor her parents wanted her to be in any way different from the other little children she would find there.

For her hat, which was to be brown, was taken the wool of eighty sheep, full grown, which was made into felt and moulded to her size; a ribbon of yellow ochre corded silk, one metre wide and 30 yards in length, was set aside to trim this hat.

Of her underwear, Mavis had 3 sets made, that is, 3 vests styled in the fashion, and 3 pairs of under or nether pants, and for these Mavis ordered that each pair should have a silk bow of pink ribbon, one foot wide and 4 metres long, for Garganette was becoming vain and Mavis wished to please her. Also with the under garments, were made 3 cotton shirts in a cream colour, with long sleeves to the wrist and a button down collar. The buttons for her shirts were specially made discs, the size of serving plates with holes put in, and the cotton for the undergarments and shirts together comprised the entire crop of cotton for an area in the Southern United States of America being not less than 30001 hectares in diameter. The silk tie, in diagonal stripes of yellow and brown, was a model of ingenuity.

Her gymslip, in brown, was made of so much material that, when they spread it out to cut the pattern, it covered 3 counties, and it will be enough to say that her blazer, with the school ensign in brown and gold on its breast pocket, silk lining and all, weighed just over 4 tonnes, while her overcoat, the belt of which was 100 metres long, weighed with the buttons and buckle, 13 cwt.

The socks, which were of a buff colour and made by the ancient acrylic process of which nothing is now known, were each long enough to put a tube train in, so that Garganette, had she found one there would have thought it was Christmas.

The shoes and satchel, which had to be of leather, presented no difficulty at all, for they simply sent for the hides of two bull elephants, one each for the shoes, and three hippopotami for the satchel, all of which were tanned and dyed to the regulation colours, that is brown for the shoes and yellow for the satchel.

Of course, all this was not done without expense, and it became necessary for Paul to re-mortgage the farm, which he did with a glad heart, as he was pleased to do any little thing for his sweet Garganette; and the work involved was so great that for the four months leading up to the middle of September the unemployment figures were reduced by so much that the national economy was in grave danger of collapse, for things never happen in isolation, and what one does affects the other, and then the next and so on until from one man swatting a fly which annoys him a whole empire might be lost, but I believe they did things differently in Garganette's time and lost their empires in other and quite different ways. But national disaster was averted, for on the night before the school opened the last stitch was sewn, the hands were laid off and all returned to normal.

Other Equipment Garganette Was Provided With For Her First Day At School

Garganette's shoe laces were made of regulation size lead piping, that is eight centimetres thick and 100 yards long, which laces she was warned on no account to suck, and her handkerchief was made of bleached linen and was as long and as wide as the farm's long meadow.

She carried with her also her sports equipment of white gym shoes, dark blue cotton knickers, 1 pr baggy white socks and a T shirt. Also her pencil case with one lead pencil and one each of blue, yellow, green and red, these all being made of full-grown Norwegian pine trees, with the branches and bark removed, seasoned and filled; one orange pencil sharpener and a 6" rule.

35

Also in her satchel she carried two gross of apples and 2 full churns of fresh cow's milk, this being for her morning snack, while lunch, in view of the size of the Ettin family, was naturally provided free. She took with her the smallest of her favourite teddy bears and, of course, her pocket calculator.

Thus was Garganette fully prepared and equipped for her new life at school, and Mavis was entirely satisfied that no one would be able to distinguish her child from any of the other little girls and so find fault with her on that account.

How Garganette Went To School

Garganette woke up and dressed herself in her new uniform, which was:
her white vest and the new underpanties with the pink bows;
a yellow shirt and a brown skirt;
yellow socks and brown shoes;
a yellow and brown tie;
a yellow hat and a brown blazer;
and a new yellow leather satchel.

It seemed to her right and proper that she should be dressed in these fundamental colours, and she was very excited and happy. All the children wore the same, because it was felt that none should stand out from the others but that all should be exactly the same, and Garganette knew that her uniform was perfectly correct and that she could not possibly stand out from the other children in any way at all.

So it was that she set out for her first day at school in the company of all her brothers and sisters, with a light heart and a serious mind. In order to get there she had to walk to the end of her father's farm, cross the village and walk down by the stream; cross the railway lines and the motorway and just a few miles further on was the dear little school where she was to spend so many happy hours and years learning facts, figures and how to be a grown-up.

It was an entirely uneventful journey until she got to the motorway when, quite without being aware of the danger, she stepped right into the middle of the fast or outside lane, and a car hit her smartly in the ankle. Poor child, she sat down in the road and wept and howled, for the shock had quite taken her good humour away, and when she saw the skin on her lower leg was broken and the good red blood was pouring out, she was inconsolable, thinking in her innocence, that she would probably come out of the hole in her leg and that would be the end of her. The noise she made howling and wailing drowned out the screeching of tyres, the dreadful crunching sounds as car hit car and the fearsome screams of the motorists as they saw eternity yawning before them. Several hundred vehicles were involved in this, the worst motorway pile-up ever recorded, and it just goes to show that one should always leave enough space between one's own front bumper and the rear end of the car ahead, to enable one to stop in an emergency without crashing. Of course, if the driver of the car behind does not also leave sufficient space, then one will be hit anyway in the event of said emergency, but the man in the car behind is always responsible, so that you won't have to pay your own funeral expenses, which is a great comfort when one is about to meet one's maker on the motorway, I'm sure.

However, eventually her siblings were able to persuade Garganette that she would be late for her first day at school and the teacher would be cross and upset and would not like to listen to excuses, nor be likely to accept any excuses offered, so she'd better hurry up, and she, sweet child, did as she was told and suffered herself to be led away, while the motorists sorted themselves out as best they could. This took several hours, as can be imagined, but they were assisted in their efforts by the police, fire brigade, ambulance service and the armed forces, who had to be brought in as the scale of the problem was quite large, really, but they did sort it out and by the time Garganette came home, it was all cleared away and, so quick was she at learning her lessons, that she jumped clean over the motorway, and never once has she since set foot on such a road.

Garganette At School

After her momentous journey, Garganette and all the other boys and girls were brought into the great assembly hall, where they were addressed by the Head Teacher, Mr Butskill, whom Garganette thought must be God, for the other children behaved towards him with great reverence and respect and besides he spoke in such a kindly and gentle manner, had such a sad and benign smile upon his face and his eyes seemed to hold all the tears ever shed. This gracious being spoke to them in the following terms:

"Good morning, children," he said, "as this is the first day of school for some of you and the first day of a new term for the rest of you, I want to talk to you about a very important matter and that is that: All Children Are Equal.

"No child is any better or worse than any other child; we make no distinction between boys and girls or between those from different age groups, races, religions or those from different social backgrounds from ourselves. We do not compete with each other, but we work together co-operatively for the good of all. Remember, children, the school motto, which is: the Whole is Greater than the Sum of the Parts.

"Finally, dear children, I want you to remember that we wear our school uniform with pride, because it marks us out as equal children from a School that bravely carries the banner of Equality.

"Now, let us sing to God, whoever She may be."

The Song They Sang To God

I Dear God, we know You love us,
    To You we always pray.
    Please make us colour blind because
    All little children are grey.

II We work for one another:
    We try just like we should
    To truly live for each other,
    Always we want to be good.

III Dear God, You are our Mother,
    And our dear Father, too;
    Please keep us all just like each other
    To show how much we love You.

What Garganette Did At School

Garganette learned all about numbers and words; how to read and to write; how to sing and to swim; she learned how to run and to jump; how to skip and to play all manner of games with balls, other sports and extra-curricular activities. She learned manners and how to address her teachers; she learned about God and how to ask Her for things. She learned everything that was put before her to learn and a lot more besides. And she never even knew she was learning.

How Garganette Did At School

She excelled.

How Garganette Excelled In Everything She Did At School

Despite all her teachers could do or say, Garganette could add up faster, divide longer, multiply more complexly and subtract more completely than any of her fellows. She could read more fluently, write more legibly and spell more correctly; she knew more words and the names of more things, more colours than there were even in the rainbow; she knew the names of all the countries and where they were; she could recite the names of all the Kings and Queens there have ever been, all the Prime Ministers and chief Revolting Peasants, and give their dates; she identified, with faultless precision, all the birds, bugs, flowers, trees, shrubs and animals, and was learning the names of the fishes.

In addition, she sang louder, jumped higher, ran faster, swam wetter than any of the other children, and in team sports she was always by popular demand the captain. She tirelessly championed the weak and was the scourge and dread of all the bullies. She got higher marks and more gold stars than ever recorded before or since, and everybody loved her.

How Mr Butskill Reacted To Garganette's Excellence

Mr Butskill walked one morning in the playground, his expression gentle and benign as ever; he watched the children at play and his wistful smile of pure love was a reassuring sign to all who could see him; he fairly shone with good nature and calm charm. He sighed with the weight of the burden on his shoulders: so many young lives given into his care and charge; so many hearts commended to his care; so many souls to guard against all the possible ills that may befall them. He spoke to them often of the way they should live their lives to be at one with each other, the world and with God, whoever She may be. He counselled them as to the proper path to take and what line to pursue in all their little difficulties; and he never missed an opportunity of correcting their errors, great and small, and putting the children back on the right road. He was the Monarch of the Little Kingdom, the Supreme Being in that Demi-Paradise, and he felt his responsibilities keenly.

He stumbled over a small weeping child. "Why Mary, whatever is the matter?", he asked rubbing his knee which had come into contact with the little hard head.

"Waaa!" cried Mary, "Tommy and Jack won't let me play with them."

"Tommy and Jack," said Mr Butskill, "why won't you let Mary play with you?"

"Oh, we don't want her, sir, she's a girl," said Tommy.

"O, Tommy, Tommy," said Mr Butskill, in evident pain at the display of harsh cynicism. "We don't say nasty things like that about people, now do we?"

"But, sir, please, sir," said Jack, "she *is* a girl, sir."

"I'm not, am I, sir?" said Mary.

"Children, children," said the saintly Mr Butskill, "you have so much to learn. Please remember how upset God will be to see you fighting."

"But, sir," said Tommy.

"Child, child," murmured Mr Butskill, the Holy Water of Grief springing to his eyes as he remonstrated with them. "You mustn't, you really mustn't make me so unhappy."

"Oh, sir, please sir, sorry sir," said the children.

"Dear little children," said Mr Butskill, beginning to smile again, "what have I told you that God says about little children?"

"God says that all little children are equal, sir," they chorused.

"And what is the School Motto?" enquired Mr Butskill, kindly.

"The greater the sum the bigger the parts, sir," they said.

"There, there, good children. Carry the banner of Equality fearlessly and with pride," said Mr Butskill, that great pedagogue, smiling with benign graciousness upon his charges as he left them.

"Alright," said Jack. "What shall we play?"

"Lets play rapists," said Mary.

"How do you play that?" asked the boys.

"Come on, I'll teach you," said Mary

Mr Butskill progressed around the playground, heading for his office by the long route. Each time he saw even the tiniest shootlet of inequality poking its head out of the fertile soil of childish minds, with gentle firmness and great ruthlessness, he pulled it out by its roots. Musing on the great and heavy task before him, and congratulating himself upon his success within the Kingdom he ruled with such firmness, he at last reached his sanctum, and began to check the reports handed in by the teachers, troops in the battle he constantly fought and was determined to win, against the scourge of inequality.

Mr Butskill, that paragon of secular and religious virtue, was satisfied by what he read. He found the most pleasing evidence of mediocrity in the children he had in his care. Little Tommy was doing well in cookery, little Mary was making steady progress with her gardening, Jack was filling out nicely. Each child was good at something, and it was his job to ensure that the seeds of ability should come to fruition, in a spirit of generous co-operation and thoughtfulness. Mr Butskill sighed with gratitude to the god that he felt sure was there somewhere, while realising that it didn't matter if she wasn't, and read on.

But what was this? Garganette Ettin had top marks in Spelling! Top marks in Reading!! Top marks in Writing!!! Top marks in Arithmetic!!!! Top marks in Co-operative Learning!!!!! And now he came to think about it, Mr Butskill remembered that Garganette Ettin was Bigger than everybody else, too!!!!!! What could it mean? What should he do about it?? The child was clearly trying, and he hoped not deliberately, to undermine his life-long attempt to instil the proper spirit of humility and equality in the hearts and minds of as many of the little children,

42

those future adults, as came within his care and control.

Mr Butskill clutched at the region around his heart. All his work ruined. Never! He would fight off this threat. There had, after all, been the other case when the little boy had insisted on being so good at jumping that he not only beat his fellows in competition, but had gone so far as to become an Olympic Silver Medalist. Mr Butskill had been able, after much soul searching and inquiry, to find a place for that child at the Special School, surely more suitable for a child with so criminal an ability to excel? He would find somewhere for this Garganette Ettin, too, somewhere she would be happier, where she could be properly looked after and contained. But first he must see the child and talk to her, for this was clearly his duty, and he must not fail.

How Mr Butskill Tried To Persuade Garganette Of The Error Of Her Ways

Mr Butskill, after due care and deep consideration of the problem, called Garganette into his room, and wishing to prove to her by logical methods that she was not doing as well as she might be doing, addressed her in the following terms:

"Dear child," he said, with an air of regal and menacing benignity, "we have talked often about God, whoever She may be, and how She loves all little children, especially those who work hard to maintain the spirit of Equality that we, in this School, wish to foster, haven't we, Garganette?"

"Oh, yes, sir," said Garganette, "you've often told us about God and what She wants."

"And in our discussions," continued Mr Butskill, "we have always agreed that, in accordance with God's wishes and under the Banner of Equality, we will try our best to work together Co-operatively, to be friends and always to be kind to each other, isn't that so, child?"

"Yes sir," said Garganette enthusiastically. "You mentioned it to us on the first day of term and you've often spoken of it since."

"Now Garganette," said Mr Butskill, his tone at once firm and rather sad, "I'm glad you have remembered and understood our talks, but it makes it all the more difficult for me to understand why you continually and consistently disregard our Policy of Co-operation and Equality."

"Why, sir," said Garganette, puzzled. "Whatever can you mean?"

"Child, child," said Mr Butskill, sternly and with tears impending, "just think a moment, reflect on your conduct over the time you've spent with us: is there not something that you should have done but have not done?"

Garganette reflected a moment, as instructed by the masterful Mr Butskill, on her career to date. Her eyes grew bigger and bigger with the effort, she swelled visibly, particularly around the area where she kept her thinking brains, so that her head became truly magnificent in size, but she couldn't think of anything she should have done but hadn't.

"Well, sir," she said at last, "I really can't think of anything."

"Under our care and guidance," said Mr Butskill, "you have had ample opportunity, just as all the other children here, to be truly Equal, but I'm very much afraid to say that you have not managed to live up to the expectations we had of you. Indeed, I almost feel it is I who have failed," and he sighed deeply, with true feeling, "and it makes me very sad. However, I will give you another chance. Today is Friday. Next week is the last week of the year, and we have our Sports & Open Day with Prize Giving & Speeches. Over the weekend I want you to think the matter through and I hope that you will come back on Monday with a better understanding of what is required of you and will be more amenable to our methods here. Otherwise..." and he sighed again from the very pit and bottom of his heart.

"But sir," said Garganette, very puzzled and quite failing to understand what he wanted from her. "I will of course think, but please give me some idea of what you want me to think about. I mean, can you be a little more specific?"

"Garganette Ettin," said Mr Butskill, "I have tried to be patient with you, and I feel that perhaps you are deliberately failing to understand what I have said to you. But, yet, you are a child and I must give you the benefit of the doubt. That is my duty, but I must say it is a hard one. See here," and he reached out for the reports. "You have top marks in all the subjects you have taken. Is that true to the spirit of Equality? What will all the other little children feel on Parents Day when you receive all the prizes? What would happen if all the children were good enough to receive all the prizes? And think how miserable their parents will be, and they will not be able to believe in and trust in me and our great work of Equality and Co-operation. All that disappointment, of parents and little children alike will be hard to bear. But that's not all, is it?"

"Isn't it?" said Garganette.

"No indeed," said Mr Butskill with great firmness and decision. "There is the matter of God and Her love for the little children. How will She feel when She looks down from Her great Paradise and sees that one child is taking all the credit which should be Equally shared by all the children, and when She sees which child, She will be sure that She is being mocked. God loves all little children, but Garganette, you have flouted Her wishes even in this matter: you are not even humble enough to be little, but must flaunt your enormous height and girth, so that God will be ashamed to think She made you.

"Think about all this, Garganette. If you come back on Monday and can prove you are sorry for what you have done, and try to be a little smaller every day, then we will see what can be done to forgive you. If not, well, I'm afraid that we will not any longer be able to find room for you in this school."

How Garganette Went Home And Reflected On The Advice Given Her By The Saintly Mr Butskill

Garganette was very shaken by the information given her by Mr Butskill, but because she trusted him implicitly, she wanted to consider what he had said in a true and proper spirit.

She refused all food offered her by Mavis, who it can be imagined was perplexed by this, and put out in her catering arrangements. Instead of eating, Garganette went straight to her room and gazed at herself in the long mirror. Then she went and brought the tallest of her brothers, Mick, to see his reflection and her own together, but when they stood in front of the mirror side by side, she couldn't see him at all. So she stood behind him and realised for the first time that she was indeed much bigger all round than even Mick, whom she had hitherto regarded as being very large.

She sat and thought and decided that she must try to be smaller, however much effort it cost her. She lay down and screwed up her face, and grunted and groaned with the effort. Then she looked in the mirror again, but there was no change, except that she was pale and greyish in colour.

"Oh dear, oh dear," she thought. "Whatever shall I do?"

All night and all the next day she lay on her bed sweating and groaning, assailed by tiny doubts and sharp little anxieties which scuttled about pricking and pinching her.

Mavis was seriously worried by her baby's inexplicable behaviour: refusing food and comfort; not laughing and singing; not playing or running around; not studying; not EATING! Not even the daintiest morsels that Mavis could prepare in the way of nourishment would she eat, and all the funniest stories told her by the other children failed to make her even smile. Mavis couldn't stand it.

"Garganette," she said, "you must eat or you will fade away. Look, I've made you a lovely beef pie. I've used three whole cows, and two sheep for the extra fat, along with a dozen hens and a duck or two for the flavour, besides the vegetables and pastry. And for afters, I've made you a wonderful Summer Pudding, almost as big as this room. Do eat something.

But Garganette sighed and shook her head.

"Garganette," said Mavis, trying not to panic. "Who will eat all this food if you don't? It will go to waste and then what will happen?"

But Garganette only turned her head away.

"Garganette," said Mavis, beginning to be very sad, "if you don't eat, you will die, and then what will I do?"

"Oh, mummy," said Garganette, her voice barely above a whisper, which is to say that she could be heard only as far as the village and no further, "if I die, will I go to God?"

"Yes Garganette," said Mavis sobbing a little.

"Oh,mummy,I'd like to see God,but I'm afraid God won't want to see me."

"Why ever not?" asked Mavis.

But Garganette closed her eyes again and sighed very, very deeply.

How Garganette Had An Entertaining And Iluminating Dream

Garganette fell asleep at last and had a long and fascinating dream.

She found herself in a strange and beautiful place. There was a magnificent forest with the most lovely trees of all kinds growing in great profusion. A myriad brightly coloured flowers bloomed together in a wild and exciting array, while insects of an amazing variety buzzed and hummed amongst them. On the lush and verdant plain were all kinds of animals, and though Garganette had top marks in naming the animals and though she knew all of them, she was surprised to see hundreds she had never even imagined before. She walked in this extraordinary and lively place and as she got nearer she began to see people. And what people they were!

There were tall people, some nearly as tall as she, with long shanks and long flanks, long hands, and one man had a thing hanging down to his knees; there were little small people, all dainty and neat, perfect in every detail, so sweet she could have eaten them; there were round fat people, with great broad bums and quivering hams, globular bellies and vast accoutrements, one woman had breasts as big as two moons with huge juicy nipples, which Garganette saw. There were athletes and dancers, all muscles and sinews, with strong supple bodies and talkative legs; small men who were strong and big men who were weak; fat women with grace and a few without; there were wild and cultivated people; young and old; children and adults; well groomed and careless; there were slim ones, fat ones, grizzled, gnarled and straight ones; lithe ones, strong ones, sighing and upright, stooping and smiling; some waved their arms around, some danced and some ran, some sat quietly, others strode noisily. And all this vast, shimmering, glowing, moving, sparkling mass of people was very excited about something and very busy. They all talked, Garganette could hear their voices but could not distinguish their words, and they touched each other, seeming to marvel and be delighted.

Then they noticed her.

"Oho! You're a fine splendid girl!" said a man with curling hair and big strong arms.

"What a dear sweet enormous giant of a little girl," said a woman, with eyes like diamonds and a sparkling face. "Where have you come from?"

"Well, I think I'm probably asleep and dreaming," said Garganette, who was a truthful child. "But I am fascinated by this place. Please tell me what you are doing here, and what you are all so excited about. I must say, you seem to be very pleased and happy, as I was before my talk with Mr Butskill."

"Oh, Mr Butskill," they said, and they looked at each other

shaking their heads. "Well, you won't find him here."

"No, I should think not," said a little tiny girl with a deep rich voice.

"You know, I think you're the tallest child we've seen here," said a big young man who had been doing double back somersaults, and everyone else agreed enthusiastically. They began to admire her and congratulate her on having such total largeness; they complimented her on her beauty and asked if she were also a clever child. They inspected her with deep attention and generous curiosity, and were, it seemed, overwhelmed with delight in her.

"Please tell me what this place is," said Garganette, who did not feel in the least shy.

"This is the Land of Equality," they told her.

"But," said Garganette, most surprised, "you're all so different from each other!"

"You've noticed!" they cried in great delight, and admired her perspicacity. "You won't find two people here alike. Even the Twins. Twins, Twins, come here to the giant Garganette and tell her about yourselves."

Two very pretty young women came up then, each so exactly like the other that Garganette was instantly confused, and it seemed to her that the people had lied to her about everyone here being different.

"I suppose you think that we're completely identical," said one, "everyone does, but we're not, we're quite different. I am fierce, though I am so pretty. I would dare to steal the sun from the sky, if I wanted to," she boasted and the company around nodded, for it was true. "I would kill anyone, however large and powerful, who tried to hurt me or someone I loved, and though I don't necessarily claim it would be right, and might even regret it afterwards, I would do it just the same and think about it later. Your Mr Butskill, I would trample underfoot, if he insulted me as he's insulted you, and then I would dance all night with as many lovely men as I could find, to celebrate my defence of freedom!"

49

All the people cheered and applauded, and Garganette wanted to go to war at once, for the fun of the thing. Then the other Twin spoke.

"Yes, I love dancing too," she said. "Dancing is beautiful, and I look for beauty everywhere, with my hands and ears, eyes and legs and my whole body. I love to swim and to run, to sing and to laugh, or to sit quiet and watch the joy around me. Oh, I see the ugliness too, but I foster freedom and fight for it by searching out and promoting the lovely, the sublime and the beautiful. As for Mr Butskill, I'd pat him on the head and try to make him laugh, because everyone looks better when they're happy, but I certainly wouldn't take any notice of what he says!"

At this the people sighed with longing and nodded agreement, for what this Twin said about herself was also true, and Garganette had a sudden inspiration and yearning for beauty.

"I see," she said, "that you are all different, even these Twins have their different ways, but I still don't understand how you can also be equal. Please explain this to me, because I would like to have it sorted out before I wake up."

"You see," said a man with an especially endearing smile, "we come here to see each other's differences, to explore each other, to learn and get to know one another. It's our chief delight and entertainment, for in discovering each other's differences is our proof of equality."

"But what if people want to be the same?" asked Garganette.

"Who'd want to be the same?" asked one Twin.

"And anyway they can't be," said the other.

"It's not possible," said a woman with elegant hands, "or at least in all our generations of study it's never happened. You mustn't confuse equality with sameness. You see, the sign of equality lies in everyone's right to be different and special."

"Of course!" cried Garganette, delighted to understand. "How wonderful! I can't wait to tell Mr Butskill about it, he'll be so pleased!"

"Tell him about Linguistic Philosophy," someone said, but

Garganette scarcely heard, for she was distracted by a movement in the sky. Looking up, she saw God, in whose hands a million different things were forming: a million kinds of grasses; insects in a diversity of form that was bewildering; a delightfully various multitude of living things, each one unlike the next, that fell to earth and took up space. God smiled and waved to Garganette, and she smiled and waved back.

Then suddenly she was awake: it was morning and she was very, very hungry.

How Garganette Answered Mr Butskill

Garganette leapt out of bed, feeling extremely well.

"Mummy! Mummy!" she called to Mavis. "May I have some breakfast, please?"

"Of course, darling. What would you like?" said Mavis, delighted that Garganette was herself again, that is all pink, shiny and splendidly healthy and large.

"That beef pie you told me about, with the three cows and sheep and things. I wouldn't want it to go to waste. And I'll take the summer pudding with me for my mid-morning break. Mmm," she said when she'd finished the pie, "that was lovely, thank you, mummy." Then she drank 21 gallons of orange juice, kissed her parents, took up her satchel and ran off to school.

On her way, she considered deeply what she would say to Mr Butskill, and turning the dream over in her mind, she remembered that someone had said something just before she noticed God in the sky. Now, what had they told her to mention to Mr Butskill? Ah, yes, Linguistic Philosophy. H'm, she thought, knitting her brows as she pondered.

Mr Butskill was waiting for her at the school.

"Well, Garganette," he said, "I'm glad you're early. Come in, and we'll hear what you've decided over the weekend. Now then," he said when they were settled in his office, "have you thought over what we talked about last week?"

"Oh yes, Mr Butskill," she said.

"And what conclusions have you reached?" he asked, with stern kindliness. "Are you going to try very hard to be Equal, as we agreed, or will you be going to another school?"

"Oh no, sir," said Garganette, "I don't want to go to another school, I love it here."

"Yes, it is a lovely School," said Mr Butskill sincerely, "but you have to prove to me that you will do everything to follow our principles of Equality."

"Oh yes, sir," said Garganette, her eyes shining with enthusiasm, "I want to do that very much. It's very interesting!"

"What?" said Mr Butskill, who didn't understand.

"Equality, sir," said Garganette. "You see, I've been thinking very hard about what you said, and I realize now that the sign of equality lies in everyone's right to be different."

"What!" cried Mr Butskill, aghast. "You haven't been thinking for yourself, have you?!"

"And the difficulty arises when people confuse equality with sameness," she continued, "for really, you know, everyone is different. Everything is different."

"What!!" shouted Mr Butskill.

"Oh yes, really," said the child earnestly, speaking up, "everything in the world. I mean, look at the extraordinary variety. Think of how many different kinds of plants there are, for instance. Or the insects! Why, we don't even know yet how many kinds of insects there are. And they're all different. And as for the variety with us humans, why it would be impossible to calculate!"

"WHAT!!!" roared Mr Butskill.

"Mr Butskill," she said, and she kindly spoke a little louder, "it is very easy to confuse the meanings of words, you know. Equality means the right to be different, to be special, to be oneself, and it seems to me, that 'same' means impossible, with regard to people, that is. You see?"

52

Mr Butskill sat and stared at her quietly, having roared all the stuffing out of himself.

"This problem of syntax has occupied philosophers for many years," continued Garganette, thoughtfully, "they call it Linguistic Philosophy and it's very important. Perhaps you would like to go on a course? They have some excellent courses at the university. Look, I've brought Daddy's Sunday papers, he won't mind, he never reads them, and there are lots of advertisements recommending study groups and training sessions," and she showed him where she'd ringed the interesting ones. "Mind you," she added as he took the papers from her, "I can't help thinking that there must be more to philosophy than mere syntax, but then, I'm only five years old and really can't be expected to know everything yet, can I?"

"I beg your pardon," murmured Mr Butskill, as one awakening from a reverie.

"Perhaps," said the child, brightening from her momentary philosophical doubts, "you could teach us when you get back from your course. That would be so nice, wouldn't it?"

"Yes," said Mr Butskill, meekly.

"And I promise you that I'm going to be as equal as I can be in my own special way," said Garganette, very seriously.

"Good girl," said Mr Butskill. "Equality, that's the thing. I think," he added doubtfully, and he felt a strange buzzing in his head and a ringing in his ears.

"Now," said Garganette, "I must go and see if the boys have come to school yet, because I want very much to discover and explore their differences with them. Bye, Mr Butskill!"

How Garganette Proved Herself Equal
During Sports & Open Day,
With Prize Giving & Speeches

Sports & Open Day was very exciting for Garganette, and she had many wonderful adventures: there were running, jumping and swimming races; track and field events galore; individual and team sports. All the children worked harder than usual, because they knew there was going to be a marvellous feast in the Great Assembly Hall after Prize Giving & Speeches, and they wanted to build up an appetite, but Garganette worked especially hard, for she was filled with the joyful spirit of equality and wanted to be sure of every prize she won.

In the high jump, for instance, she leapt so high that she touched the moon on her first attempt, and vowed as she came back to earth, that she would reach Mars next time; in the long jump she jumped so far that she jumped right round the world three times, a most exhilarating experience. As to the swimming, well, she...

What? You don't believe me? Really? Well, I can assure you that I had it from the written account of the eminent historian Wattsisnaim; an Article Published in a Newspaper, and you know he never lies. And what's more, he was definitely there, because he has an especial interest in sports. So you see, if you don't believe me you must check with him.

"I will," he said.

Now, where was I? Ah, sports. Well, Garganette won them all, except the tennis, which she lost on a technicality, for the force with which she hit the ball sent it spinning off into the fifth dimension and, as it couldn't be recovered thence, she forfeited the match.

Then all the parents and children were called in to the Great Assembly Hall and were addressed by the Vicar, who was to give the prizes, from the stage. There were prizes in all categories, that is: Academic Achievement; Sporting Activity; Good Conduct; Cleanliness, and Special Merit.

Garganette won prizes for Excellence in the following subjects:

Reading	Writing
Spelling	Addition
Subtraction	Multiplication
History	Division (long & short)
Naming the Plants	Naming the Animals
Naming the Places	Naming the People
Fractions	Decimals
Trigonometry	Biology
Chemistry	Geography
Geology	Demography
Russian	Aramaic
Urdu	Bengali
Latin	Greek (which it was to her)
Persian	Swahili
Singing	Dancing
Jumping	Running
Shining	Sparkling
Anatomy	Theology
Microbiology	Etymology
Philosophy	Cordiality
Mandarin (Chinese)	Eating
Drinking	Laughing
Spitting	Drawing
Shitting	Pissing
Dreaming	Height
Music	Composition
Special Projects	Tall Stories
Yarn Spinning	Fancy Weaving
Mandarin (Oranges)	Logical Positivism
Ergonomics	Economics
Liberal Studies	Humanities
Comparative Religions	Group Dynamics
Philosophy & Economics	Philosophy of Economics
Economics of Philosophy	Law

and two Special Prizes, that is: one for Size and the other for Excellence; and a third for Health and a fourth for herself.

The Vicar called each prize winner to the stage, where he handed out the Prize and gave a little Speech, such as, "Well done, Mary. Here's your Prize," and Mary replied, "Thank you very much, sir," and returned to her seat, all red in the face from shyness and being pleased. Garganette received in prizes 18,000 copies of "The Story of God, Whoever S/He May Be, for the Younger Reader" from the Vicar, and a great roar of approval and ringing, resounding cheers from everyone else. She gave the books to her father, Paul, who kept one as a memento and sold the rest at a modest profit; but the cheers she kept in her soul forever.

Then there was the great bean feast, with enormous eating and drinking, and a bun fight. Everyone ate as much, laughed as much, talked as loudly and showed off as much as they possibly could, until they were all almost fit to burst with eating, merriment and feeling pleased with themselves.

So it was that Garganette proved herself equal by winning as many prizes as she could, and on the last day of the last term of her first year at school she said to her friend and teacher, Mr Butskill, "My special kind of equality is to be good at everything. Isn't life wonderful?"

"Yes indeed," said Mr Butskill, and after he'd waved everyone goodbye and locked up the school, he hurried off to the university, where he had enrolled in a course, as suggested by his friend and teacher, Garganette, in Linguistic Philosophy, "For," as he said to himself on the way, "there must be something in it."

How Garganette Grew Up

The years passed, season followed season in the regular way and Garganette progressed from the Little School in the village, with every honour heaped upon her, to the Big School in the town, which barely had room to accommodate her, going from strength to strength, always at the forefront of any activity, pushing back the frontiers of knowledge, informing her teachers, teaching her grandmother to suck eggs, learning everything that there was to learn. She continued to grow, not only in body which is to be expected of a child, but in the acquisition of facts, also, to such an extent that it was astonishing to the casual passer-by confronted by such true knowledge and learning, such a giant collection of facts. She could answer any question asked of her on any or all of the following subjects:

Geography	Demography
Calligraphy	Typography
Historiography	Biography
Telegraphy	Photography
Iconography	Ethnography
Logography	Hagiography......

We interrupt this list to bring you the news that Garganette has just awoken to find blood everywhere! Blood on the carpet, blood on the bed, blood round her ankles and up to her head; blood on the ceiling, blood on the floor, blood on the desk and still there's more.

Our Special Correspondent has just phoned through with his report and he's on the line now. What's happening, Ted?

It's incredible, Tom! There's blood everywhere! Gallons of it! I've never seen anything like it! Coming up to the farm where Garganette lives with her family, I was met by a great bloody flood, oozing down from the farm house and on its way to engulf the village. As I look behind me now towards the village,

I can see blood as far as the horizon. It's INCREDIBLE!!! There's blood still pouring out of the farm house and into the yard, where Paul Ettin is standing.

Tell me, Paul, what exactly happened?

Well, Ted, I don't know. There was blood everywhere! The whole house was filling up with it, so I opened the front door quick.

And that let the blood out, did it?

That's right, Ted.

And here's Mavis Ettin. Tell me Mavis, how did you feel when you went to Garganette's bedroom and were met by a flood of blood?

Well, Ted. It's very hard to say, really. I suppose you could say it's a shock, really, coming across all that blood in your own house. I mean, I never dreamt that there could be so much blood all together like that at once.

And how is Garganette taking it?

Well, Ted, you can't tell with Garganette how she'll react. Although I must say, she's a very happy girl, normally, really.

Thank you, Mavis. We've just been told that the Home Secretary is on holiday, at the moment, but the Prime Minister will be visiting later this morning. And we've now been joined by the Chief Constable, the Chief Ambulance Driver and the Chief Fire Officer. Tell me, sir, how do you react to this?

Well you know, Ted, we do expect this sort of thing from young girls of this age, I mean it's only to be expected, isn't it? But I must say that Garganette really takes the biscuit!

Do you see any danger arising out of a situation like this?

Well, Ted, I don't see any danger from this sort of thing. It happens all the time, you know, you'd be surprised. I think we've averted National Disaster this time, though I daresay that the cleaning up operation will take some time, but it's just what we'd expect, you know.

And now here is Garganette herself! Garganette, Garganette! Tell me how do you feel?

Oh, Ted, I feel great, wonderful! I never thought that having your first period would be so, well, so completely usual, if you see what I mean. I mean, it's just what you'd expect, isn't it? And everyone has been so wonderful! It's really great!

And do you think you'll do it again?

Ha ha ha, Ted! What a funny question! Of course I'll do it again! Oh, there you are, mummy, I'm starving. Can I have my breakfast, please?

Amazing! Garganette feels great! Finally, if I can ask you, Mavis, what are you going to do now?

Well Ted, I just want to put all this behind us really, and get back to normal. It takes it out of you, a thing like this.

Well, that's the story from the Ettin farm, out here in a landscape suddenly turned red overnight. It has been an incredible time for everyone but even now I can see that everything is getting back to normal, now, so this is Ted handing you back to Tom in the studio.

Thank you, Ted. And just to reassure anyone who's just tuned in: Garganette is feeling great and is now having her breakfast.

How Garganette Developed

Garganette's stomach, whichever way you approached it, was a vast and bottomless pit. When it came to eating, my goodness could she eat: for her breakfast she would have 50 boxes of cereal, with oats, nuts, raisins, fruit and other wonderful things in it; for her lunch she would insist on a spanish omelette the size of a dozen duvets, or a stew made of lamb, rabbit, venison, chicken, ducks, geese and whatever was to be caught, together with vegetables in season, all cooked up in one huge pot; sometimes on her way home from school she would go for a quick snack at the Biggest Best Beefiest Burger Bar, opened by an enterprising young man who had heard of her capacity in the food consuming line, where she ate large quantities of udder pie, tripes and other nameless animal derivatives cooked up into little, thin, flat cakes and put into buns, or she would go to the Splendid New McPizza Palazzo, opened by another enterprising entrepreneur, and ordered more plates of different tripes. Some evenings she went to both places. And that was only her meals. To ease the pangs in her belly between whiles, she scoffed crates of bread, pecks of cakes, barrels of cheese, acres of plums, bushels of chips; for her Sunday lunch she regularly had a whole herd of sheep with a field each of potatoes, onions, carrots and brussel sprouts, and her puddings were given her in a jacuzzi with the plug hole bunged up.

She became almost spherical in shape, and still she ate with such an appalling thoroughness that eventually Mavis had to say something about it.

"Garganette," she said with fearful admiration, "you're a pig."

At which Garganette roused herself from her post-prandial torpor and, brightening, said, "Ooooh lovely, bacon for breakfast. Oh, Mummy, I love you!" and she wrapped little Mavis in a great squashy bear hug.

"Oh, get away with you," said Mavis, flustered by this display of affection, "Now run along to bed."

Garganette did as she was told, and she sighed blissfully into a deep sleep, where dreams swathed her head: dreams of little, fat porkers, every one a succulent morsel, which danced laughing into the frying pan and sizzled there happily, playing with the tomatoes and mushrooms, until they were that lovely crisp golden brown colour with the fat running off them, and then they all jumped up, squealing with gladness, to leap with joyous daring, into her happy mouth; longing, these little pigs were, to fulfill their communal ambition to be at one with Garganette, while she, gentle innocent child, welcomed them and acknowledged them with deep satisfaction.

Such was her power, that at breakfast she was delighted to find her dream come true, and there on her plate were a dozen charming little pigs ready for the tooth; though it must be said that she was a little disappointed to find there were only twelve. The poor child knew nothing of moderation or restraint, for no one had ever taught her.

It will be understood by the discreet and tender reader that Garganette had reached a Certain Age, and with her dreadful rotundity of form, she also developed a range of spots so diverse of kind and alarming to see that her own family could no longer bear to look upon the hitherto lovely aspect of its Greatest Member, and avoided direct touch of her or anything belonging to her. Garganette was indeed an Object almost too hideous even to write about, but in my capacity of Official Biographer, I will do my best to render in words a picture of the Fearfulness she had become.

She had spots on her head, spots on her nose, spots on her fingers, her ears and her toes; spots on her back, spots on her front, spots on her bottom, her face and her knees. Great, globular, glistening pustules, yellow, black and red, and even while she slept, more and more were bred. Huge greasy blackheads sprang up around her neck and an army of the same waited in platoons on her back. She had eczema and acne, eczemous acne and acneous eczema. She even had pimples on her dimples.

Her family drew back from her squeamishly; neighbours ran from her, afraid it might be contagious; persons of a nervous disposition avoided catching sight of her, for her appearance gave them terrible nightmares, and naughty and fractious children were warned by their mothers that, if they weren't very good and quiet, Garganette would come and get them, but none of this was noticed by Garganette, whose dearest pastime at this period of her life, next only to eating, was to sit gazing into her mirror and picking fondly at her spots, squeezing them and teasing them until they burst with loud noises, like when the lid is forced off a full paint pot, the suction making a cheerful glooping sound. She loved her spots, she gloried in them: she worried when they didn't seem really large and healthy, or as many as they had at the last time she looked, and then she was plunged into melancholy. But at other times she thought that, since she was so good at it, she would become the best spot grower in the world. She would be known as the Greater Spotted Garganette and get tremendously famous and rich; she would be the Spot Heiress and found a Dynasty of Spotitude, until in the end, she could envisage the whole world would become one huge boil which she, Garganette, would personally be invited to burst.

How Mavis Set About Curing Garganette Of Her Spots

One day Mavis said to Garganette, "Being fat is one thing and we can cope with the inconvenience of having to squeeze against the walls everytime we pass you, but the spots are too much, so I've decided to do something about it. Tomorrow we are going to the Doctor."

The doctor after careful consideration of the problem, decided that a diet would be the answer, so they tried:

a liquid diet	a starvation diet
a crash diet	a university diet
a fat free diet	a sugar free diet
a salt free diet	a vegetable free diet
a cholesterol free diet	a meat free diet
a carbohydrate free diet	a milk free diet
a vitamin free diet	a trace element free diet
a protein free diet	a calorie free diet
a liquid free diet	and a food free diet

which made Garganette so hungry that she turned feral, stealing food from the neighbouring farms and making fires on the other side of the hill to cook it on. But the neighbours complained to

Paul, so then Mavis decided they must go and see a Consultant. First they went to the Ear, Nose & Throat man, but though he spied and prodded and listened, he couldn't find any answer and had to give it up, but Mavis wouldn't give up and these are the Consultants they visited:

Neurologist
Ophthalmologist
Urologist
Gynaecologist
Cardiologist
Dwarfologist
Aromatherapist
Psychotherapist
Psychiatrist
Psychologist
Behavioural Psychologist
Educational Psychologist
Depth Psychologist
Psychoanalyst (Freudian)
Psychoanalyst (Jungian)
Psychoanalyst (Adlerian)
Psychoanalyst (Freestyle)
Alienist
Sexologist
Hypnotist
A Doctor
Another Doctor
This, That and the Other Doctor
Witch Doctor
Alternative Therapist
Masseur
Masseuse
Paediatrician
Opotherapist

Optician
Osteopath
Homoeopath
Psychopath
Pathologist
Chiropodist
Dentist
Dermatologist
Pharmacist
Physiotherapist
Herbalist
Spiritualist
Bio-Energenics Specialist
Bio-Rhythm Reader
Tea-Leaf Reader
Palmist
Guru
Water Diviner
Fortune Teller
Stargazer
Faith Healer
Layer on of Hands
Counsellor
Gestalt Counsellor
Manipulator
Priest
Vicar
Bishop
Deacon

Aversion Therapist	Arch Deacon
Art Therapist	Arch Bishop
Dietician	Arch Duke
Phrenologist	Arch Fiend
Geneticist	Pope

but despite the best efforts of all these good and learned people, Garganette still had all her spots.

How Garganette Found She Was Looking For Something

Garganette wandered lonely as a cloud, and on her face a host, a crowd of golden yellow spots. Passing by a great oak tree, she saw her shoe lace was undone and, fearing she might trip up and land with a thump, she knelt to tie it and thus came face to face with a splendid little robin red breast.

"Oh, hullo, Robin!" she said, delighted to see him.

"Hullo, Garganette," said the Robin, "what are you looking for?"

"Am I looking for something?" asked Garganette.

"Of course," said he, "you're searching so hard that your very insides are trying to get out and find it."

"What do you mean?" asked Garganette.

"Why, all those fine spots of yours. That's you searching, that is."

"Is it?" asked Garganette. "But what am I searching for?"

"For the mystery!" said he.

"What mystery?" said she.

"Well, what mysteries are there?" said the Robin.

"Well," said Garganette, "let's think. There's -

Who made me?
and
Was it fun?

64

and
Who made the world?
and
How was it done?
and
What is life?
and
Who is God?
and
Where is Heaven?
and
Where did the Robin get his sweet red breast?
and
What is love?
and
Why is life?
and
How is beauty?
and
Where is truth?
and
What is death?
and
Is there a point?
and
Why do I tremble?
and
What don't I know?
and
Who made God?
and
Shall I really die?
and
What will happen then?
and

Will I be born again?
and
Will I remember you?
and
Will you remember me?
and
Will you always love me?
and
Shall I miss you?
or
Shall I die too?
and
How does a fish live in water?
and
Why did we learn to breathe air?
and
How did we learn to walk?
and
Who invented language?
and
Who taught him?
and
Were Adam and Eve?
and
Why do birds fly?
and
How do cats purr?
and
Why do dogs bark?
and
Whence is pain?
and
What is ill?
and
How is well?

66

and
How much is nature?
and
How much is nurture?
and
What is genetic inheritance?
and
Who is deviant?
and
Will I?
and
Will you?
and
Can they?
and
Should she?
and
Why he?
and
Who, me?
and
What?
and
Where?
and
When?
and
Who?
and
How?
and
Why, why, why?"

"There you are, you see," said the Robin, "all your spots are go-ing!"

"Are they?" said Garganette. "But which question am I searching for?"

"Well, I must be off now." said the Robin. "I've got something to find."

"Are you looking for something too?" said Garganette, surprised. "Do you know what it is?"

"Oh, I know what I'm looking for, alright. There aren't any spots on my red breast, are there," and he flew away, with his spotless red breast glowing like a beacon.

How Garganette Went On Certain Journeys

After this extraordinary discussion with the Robin, Garganette was left wondering what her special and particular question might be and how she was to find it, and she went on her way much puzzled as to what she should do.

As she walked she thought, and as she thought it came to her that all the answers to all the possible questions lay in heaven, for so she had been taught by Mr Butskill, and she found that she very much wanted to go there: not to stay, you understand, but to visit so that she could find out what she was searching for, and the more she thought on this new idea, the more it seemed the only solution to her immediate problem, and she almost began to fret over how she could get to heaven, for no one had ever mentioned any route save the final one, which she did not wish to take just yet for personal and private reasons, connected with the wish to live a full, happy and long life.

Now, at this critical moment in her deliberations, she saw the sun about to disappear behind a large black cloud and on an impulse followed him, for she was sure he'd guide her right. Oh, clever Garganette! Who but a child of genius could have found the other way? Her inspired guess paid off: it cost her an effort; she'd gone for gold and she felt the burn, but with one last mighty pull, her head at last was through. Her legs still dangling above the earth caused the people down below some amazement, but she hauled herself up, holding on to the two sides of the opening and by the prodigious strength of her arms was soon up and through the skies, sitting just inside the entrance of heaven.

Garganette's entry into the celestial sphere was somewhat rough and abrupt and it was some moments before she righted herself and began to take account of her surroundings. The first thing she noticed was a noise, or more accurately, a dreadful cacophony, so bad that she pressed her hands over her ears. Then she looked around and saw that she was at the tail end of a vast multitude of untold numbers of people. Then an angel appeared out of nowhere and before she could warn him, he'd crashed into her shoulder.

"Ow!" cried the angel, going into a tail spin.

"Are you all right?" asked Garganette, catching him gently before he fell into her lap.

"Garganette! What are you doing here? You're not dead, and it's not allowed, you know. Oh, my poor feathers! Look at them, they're all ruffled!" and he began to whimper.

"I am sorry," said Garganette, most contritely, "let me have a look at them."

"No, no," said the angel. "I must resign myself to whatever the good Lord sends me. Only I do think you should be more careful. What are you doing here, anyway?"

"I've come to get some answers, or rather some questions," Garganette began to explain, but the row from the crowd was so great that she couldn't even hear what she was thinking. "Oh," she said, "please tell me, what is that dreadful noise?"

"What do you mean!" cried the angel. "That's not a dreadful noise. That's the Heavenly Hosts singing His Praises. Listen!"

"HOSANNA! HOSANNA!" roared the crowd.

"Can't he teach them to sing in tune?" asked Garganette.

"Garganette, please!" cried the angel, very shocked.

"Sorry," said Garganette, who seemed to keep saying the wrong thing. "And why are they praising him?"

"Because no one is nasty to them here. No one beats them or starves them; they don't suffer poverty or humiliation or disease. They have suffered a lifetime of enslavement on earth and here they reap their reward."

"But why have they suffered so much?" asked Garganette.

"Because people are so wicked, of course."

"Why?" asked Garganette.

"Ah," sighed the angel, "it's a Mystery."

"But can't he make them good?"

"No! Well, He could, of course, but that's not His way."

"But why not?"

"Because it's a Mystery, and that's an end of the matter. Here the Miserable of the earth are free to sing His praises through all Eternity. Now, please stop asking all these adolescent questions, and tell me what you want here. I'm very busy, very busy. You've no idea how much work I have to do. Checking people in after they've got through the Gates. Preparing for the Second Coming; helping Peter with the Record Books; helping Him Himself sometimes. It's never ending! Mind you, I suppose I should be grateful that we don't deal with reincarnation here. That involves a terrible amount of administration, you know. Having to sort out who goes back as what, and where, and after how long. And it's not just people either; there's all the animals as well. I once heard about a frog that wanted to go back as a bear, and an eagle that refused to be a lion. Can you imagine! All the arguments and fuss. And the terrible scandal when they ran out of unicorns! Oh, no thank you! I'm very pleased I don't have to trouble with all that. Well, well, my feathers seem to be all right now, so I'd best be on my way. And just you be more careful next time."

"Please wait," said Garganette, "I haven't got what I came here for. You see, I'm looking for the right question."

"Oh dear," said the angel, "not more questions. We don't have questions here, only the final Mystery. Haven't you realised that? You'd better go to the other place. Hand me my clipboard

and I'll write you a pass. There now," he went on giving her an official Celestial Form, "that's your authority to travel freely in the Nether Regions. Now off you go, and mind you don't come back until you're called!" and away he flew.

"Thank you," shouted Garganette above the noise of rejoicing. "Now, how do I get there?"

How Garganette Travels Below

Glancing at the ticket the angel had given her, Garganette saw there were many routes to hell, and having narrowed the choice down to the Slippery Slope or the Primrose Path, she eventually chose the latter in honour of a certain good Doctor. It was a pleasant journey, very easy going and in almost no time she found herself being confronted by an ancient boatman on the banks of a dark river.

"Give me your gold," said he.

"I haven't any," said she.

"Then I can't ferry you over. Anyway you'd sink us, I daresay."

"Oh, that's alright," said Garganette, "I'm travelling another way," and stretching her legs she stepped over to the other side, where she was met by a fierce little growler.

"Good dog," she said, patting him on the heads. "Now which way do I go?"

She turned to the left; she turned to the right; she sniffed the air until she smelt burning, then she followed her nose and at last came to a brightly lit, dark, red place filled with hundreds of little devils, cavorting, quarrelling, squealing and squeaking, and up to all sorts of tricks: jabbing each other with prongs; tweaking each other's noses; laughing behind their hands; snivelling in corners; locking horns; lashing tails; prancing about on their little cloven hooves, and doing other things too obscene for Garganette, being young, to notice, and they were so naughty and so comical that she laughed out loud at them, so that they all stopped what they were doing and stared at her.

"Hooray!" they cried. "Someone to torment! Run quickly and tell the Evil One!" then they stood up to Garganette and said, "Come here you, and quick about it. Stop laughing and get yourself ready for torture!"

Then suddenly there was a great booming and bellowing which filled the cavernous chamber. All the little devils fell grovelling on the floor, and two goose bumps popped up on Garganette's arm in alarm.

"AH SINNER!" thundered Lucifer, "WE'RE GOING TO TOR-TURE YOU!"

"Oh no you're not," said Garganette."I'm not a sinner; I'm just travelling through. See, here's my pass."

"Oh dear," said the Fallen One. "No one comes here to stay any more. It's no fun."

"Really?" said Garganette, politely.

"Tourists!" he said bitterly. "Everyone's just passing through. As if Hell were a side show. 'Oh, Elmer, look at the Devil. Now isn't he cute.' No one's afraid any more. They just don't seem to believe in me. I don't know what to do! Mind you," he went on tentatively, glancing at her, "I've been thinking lately. I thought, you see...But you'd laugh," and he stopped, looking at her angrily.

"No, I won't laugh," said Garganette. "You're obviously hav-ing a very nasty time of it. Do tell me your idea."

"Well, I thought perhaps if we made the place more attractive, you know, jollied it up a bit. What do you think? I realise that we've got a bit of a bad reputation, but if we had a good spring-clean, wrote out a nice brochure with some really explicit photos showing what we do here, and advertised in all the right places, eh? People'll buy anything these days if it's properly advertised, won't they?"

"Oh," said Garganette, a bit taken aback by all this. "I suppose they might."

"You suppose they might," he said glaring at her. "Well," he

suddenly bellowed, "I won't compromise! I'm not selling out! I won't do it! I won't, I won't, I won't! I provide Everlasting Damnation and I do it very well, too, and if people don't want it, they can, they can, they can just not have it, so there! Anyway, what do you mean coming here and tempting me like that?"

"Oh," said Garganette, startled by his outburst. "Did I tempt you? I am sorry. I came here looking for the right question, but I'm not sure this is the best place to find it."

"No, damn it, you've definitely got the wrong place. I don't deal in questions; it's too late for that here. I hand out retribution and revenge, punishment for sinners and wrong done. Listen," he said, calming down a bit, "some people come here, some go up there, most don't really go anywhere, but some fetch up in a different zone, and you might try visiting it. It's just this way: along the path, then go up a bit, round the corner, double back twice and straight on. You can't miss it. Now, get the Hell out of here!"

"Right," said Garganette, "thank you very much," and following the fiendish directions given her, she soon found the place for which she was looking.

How Garganette's Quest Was Begun

Garganette was delighted by the land which now came into view: rolling grasslands spread out between great forests; wild flowers carpeted the earth in colourful profusion; animals gambolled and grazed, pondered and played; graceful buildings dotted the landscape, and men and women worked or strolled at ease. All was harmony within nature, all was peace and beauty. It was wonderfully lovely and she breathed in the clear fragrant air, eagerly embracing the great sense of freedom which surrounded her. At length her eyes became accustomed to the light and she spied a jovial, ancient gentleman sitting on the grass at a place where many roads met.

"Why hullo!" he said. "My name is Rabelais. How do you do?

Sit down here beside me. You're a charming wench! A powerful young woman! That's the way! Fine, fat and dimpled," and he embraced her cordially. "But you remind me enormously of a tremendous, fearsome young fellow I know of; well furnished as you are, who kept everything he had open and above board for public edification and delight. A noble little braggart, a giant among scholars, and as tall as anything you can imagine. He loved all that was lovable and knew nothing that was not!"

"You must mean my Great Grand Father Gargantua!" said Garganette, instantly recognising the portrait, "the best and grandest there ever was. Do you know him?"

"Know him? Intimately! And you're alike to him as anything I ever saw, saving significant delightful differences, and that he was taller than you; but you'll grow, you'll grow! Now, my gigantic little love, tell me all you know."

And Garganette, who felt inclined to boast and show off, cut a caper, danced a proper jig, merrily told him all she knew and all she hoped to learn, while the good old fellow laughed and slapped his thigh, asking dainty and difficult conundrums which she answered without winking once, so that their fondness for each other was very great and evident. Then at length she said: "M'sieur, tell me something. I've been everywhere today, just everywhere, and haven't got it worked out at all. Tell me, please, what question should I ask?"

"H'm," he mused. "You want a question, I see. But the question is not as important as the answer."

"Then what should the answer be?" asked Garganette, becoming very much puzzled in her head and wondering if she were to be set a new and more difficult task.

But the honest M'sieur patted her great knee and said, "Now, it shouldn't be too hard for someone with your vast resources. Do you know where you are? What this lovely country is?"

"No."

"Why, it's a library

"A library?"

"Of course, and you're in the travel section!"

"The travel section?"

"Why yes. Look here at the sign posts. See? Look, that's the way to the Republic, we're very proud of that, and close by it is the Cave, a most wonderful example. Over there lie Utopia, Erewhon and Nowhere. And yonder, across stormy seas are lands of little people and giants, though nothing at all like you, where that fool mooning over his horses has recently been. Oh, there are many fascinating places you can visit here."

Garganette was entranced by what he told her, and, wanting to hear more, said, "And what are you doing here, my dear M'sieur?"

"Ah," he said with a very proud modesty, "this beautiful land hereabouts is my place, the Monastery of Thélème. I'm just now on a visit. It is so lovely, for the motto is:

DO WHAT YOU WILL

and that is the only rule."

"It sounds wonderful," said Garganette, expressing thoughtful enthusiasm. "I should like very much to go there."

Just then there was a terrific rush of huge numbers of people who would have knocked poor M Rabelais over if he had not been shielded by the generous bulk of Garganette, who though concerned for her dear friend could hardly blame their eagerness to reach Thélème. But she was astonished to see them swerve from the road to the monastery and storm off down a completely different path.

"But where are they going?" she asked.

"To Shangri La and Never Never Land."

"And what will they find there?" she asked expecting to hear of some new marvels.

"Oh," he said, "you know; empty dreams unfulfilled, that sort of thing."

"Then why do they choose to go there instead of to Thélème?"

and the poor child wrinkled up her brow in an effort to understand the confusing ways in which people behave.

"Well, now that is a very difficult question to answer," said M Rabelais. "If you have the motto DO AS YOU WILL you have to know what you want and to decide for yourself. That is a responsibility of which people are frightened. They either want to be told what they want or else rush away into illusion."

"Is that the question we can't answer: what do people want?" asked Garganette.

"Yes, that's the question."

"And what is the answer?"

"From the question, the answer follows: the truth is what people really want. And they want the truth about themselves, because DO WHAT YOU WILL also means KNOW THYSELF."

"Why don't people know about themselves?"

"That's a very good question. They don't know about themselves because they are afraid, because they want such big things and such beautiful things and they feel they have no right, so they don't dare want it, and because they don't dare to want it they run away from the truth."

They were both quiet for a while thinking, then he went on, "There was a young poet here, they called him Byron, and he used to say, its an odd world when pleasure is a sin and sin a pleasure, and then people got confused, didn't they?" Garganette lay on the sweet grass with her chin resting on her hands, listening to her dear friend, while he leaned back against her cushioned arm, telling her these things he'd learned and, after a pause in which she savoured his wisdom, she said, "Dear M Rabelais, I'd love to visit Thélème."

How Garganette Sees The Way Other People Live

"And so you shall, my darling little pet," cried Rabelais. "Take me up in your hand and put me in your pocket, where I'll be cushioned nicely, and I can guide your steps along our route to the best place I know of."

So Garganette did as she was told and, following his directions, in a very short time they reached the Monastery of Thélème.

It was a beautiful and imposing place, built on a hexameter, with six towers and graceful arches in the old style, the sight of which pleased her greatly and made Rabelais dance in her pocket with pride. Before they went in, Garganette read the inscription above the gate, which states who may and who may not enter, to satisfy herself that she was a fit visitor. But because she was neither vile hypocrite nor bigot, puffed up swindling, pious, snivelling, scoundrelly, mock-godly ape; nor deceitful, canting, beggarly, pot-bellied villain; because she knew no violence, was not a lawyer, scribe nor pharisee, never devoured people and did not bray; and as she was neither usurious, pettifogging, tricksy, hunchbacked, nor dastardly, seditious, jealous, pox-ridden, ulcerous, scabby nor dishonoured, she took courage. And being none of these, but was instead of the highest possible lineage, and frank, fearless, definitely a flower of beauty with joy in her face, upright and modest as required, besides having other qualities which made her even more welcome here than she was in all other places, she smiled gladly and on a nod from her friend, entered in.

In the first courtyard was a glorious fountain, on top of which were three graceful ladies in white stone, from whose every orifice water was cascading. This sight pleased Garganette and while she was discussing its merits with her old friend, they were joined by the inhabitants of Thélème who welcomed them with every glad courtesy and show of honour. They were very beautiful people. The women wore scarlet stockings and crimson shoes; they had on silk taffeta gowns in blue, or orange or whatever colour took their fancy, all done over with gold embroidery and they wore jewels of exquisite stone and craftsmanship. The men, too, were richly dressed in a gorgeous, antique style, and the whole assembly presented a vivid sparkling picture to feast the eye upon.

But it was the faces and figures of the people which made the deepest impression on Garganette: there was something so gladsome and loving, so light and tender about them; they moved, for all their rich attire, with such ease and grace, and seemed to dance with every movement. Their eyes sparkled, their smiles shone, their faces beamed with light. When they spoke it was like lovely music and when they sang it was a wonder to her ears. They were the very embodiment of love, quintessentially alive, and Garganette saw how right and good it was.

They were thrilled to see Monsieur Rabelais and almost smothered him with embraces, and were generous in their affections to Garganette.

"Welcome to Thélème," they cried. "Welcome to our glad Monastery, where we worship life according to the true gospels. We will have a feast prepared for you, and while these preparations are in hand, sit down amongst us and let us tell you what you wish to know."

Now, this was all very pleasing to Garganette, for she loved to be in good company, loved to participate in feasts and, knowing she would soon be eating a good dinner, loved to ask questions and to learn, so she said:

"I know very little of monasteries, but they seem always to be austere places, where there are either only men or only women, who live hard lives, wear dull clothes and spend their time cloistered up in meditation, or else tyrannise little children whom they are meant to teach, oppressing young minds with fear of life, castigating those who love, and promising freedom only in death. Or so I've heard. But you are not like that, so why is this called the *Monastery* of Thélème?"

"Those ills you speak of do exist, we hear, and worse," came the reply, and a shudder went through the assembly at her words. "But here we worship truth, beauty, love and life, and so we are beautiful. Our founder was quite clear on this point and endowed our monastery so generously that this true worship will continue, and everything we do promotes this aim.

"Men and women live here together, for how can a woman be beautiful without men, and a man without women is only half a man.

"We dress beautifully to adorn our own beauty and in this worship the beauty of life. Do you see? Everything we do is to promote the good.

"And we have only one rule, for we are free by birth as all people are free, and we adhere closely to our law and obey it at all times, and in doing so we show our love of all that God has given us when he gave us life, and this rule, written large in our hearts and minds, is: DO AS YOU WILL and it is all the law we need."

And they fell to hugging each other and dancing, while Rabelais roared his approval and Garganette clapped her hands for joy.

Then the feast was ready. A good dinner, did I say? Garganette always expected a good dinner, but this was something else! A truly magnificent feast it was! A great overwhelming perfection of a meal! A spread to rival all others, a gigantic picnic! A rollicking gorge, a mountainous, ginormous preparation, a fabulous, rumbustious, exquisite, ding-dong of glorious proportions, the very epitome of all festivities, the exact model of banquets, and Garganette never forgot what meats there were: bear stuffed with stag stuffed with boar stuffed with goat stuffed with sheep stuffed with rabbit stuffed with hyrax stuffed with mushroom, plus a few roasted ox. And the fowl! Peacock stuffed with swan stuffed with goose stuffed with duck stuffed with chicken stuffed with partridge stuffed with pigeon stuffed with widgeon stuffed with quail stuffed with snails fed on quince. There was fish too, a dainty dish especially prepared for the guests of honour, a delightful concoction of whale which was found with a shark inside which had swallowed a dolphin which was rescuing a tuna which had harboured a great cod which was stuffed with a herring which had eaten a sprat, and the whole was basted in a fine sauce of champagne and sour cream and was most excellent to the taste.

There were salads on the side, herbs spices sauces condiments pickles aspics and other preserves without which no meal can be considered edible, and puddings, fruits, cheeses, wines and juices. And the whole menu with recipes, giving quantities and alternatives out of season, can be obtained in Garganette's excellent large book entitled, Some Meals I Have Enjoyed or The Way to a Giant's Heart (How to Feed Your Man and Make a Giant of Him) Memoirs of a Giant Appetite, which is soon to be published in hard covers and issued at a modest price.

In Which Certain Points Of Etiquette Are Raised

And when this dainty little snack was finished and the diners were lolling back wiping the grease from their chops, Garganette turned to her hosts and thanked them gratefully, saying: "You are so very kind to go to all this trouble."

"No trouble, no trouble we assure you," they replied, smiling with graceful ease.

"But all the preparation and the cooking," protested Garganette.

"Oh the cook and the kitchen staff handle everything, you know. It's all taken care of."

"A cook! Then you must let me do the dishes," exclaimed Garganette, trying to stand up, "for in my home whoever does the cooking never does the washing up."

"Oh dear!" cried the delightful young Thélèmites, blushing for her lack of noblesse. "You really mustn't stir yourself. Come, let us go into the gardens to sing. The servants will deal with all this," and the beautiful girls ran out laughing for the joy of life, while the men paused only to take up their lutes before following them.

Garganette turned to her friend.

"Servants, M'sieur Rabelais?" she said.

"Why of course, my love. You didn't think that my beautiful young ladies and gentlemen could have prepared this great feast? Or made their exquisite jewels and clothes? Or anything else, come to that!"

"But what do they do, these Thélèmites?"

"They do what they will," he replied.

"Don't they work?"

"Oh, no."

"Don't they want to work?"

"I shouldn't think so, at all. They are really not much more than children," he said indulgently. "And think how such labour would spoil their delicate loveliness."

"It's extraordinary," said Garganette. "Everyone I know works. My father, Paul, has the farm, and my mum does everything in the house, and Mr Porgie works harder than anyone. Why, even my teachers work. And, oh, M'sieur Rabelais, what about equality?"

"You must explain exactly how that fits in, my pet, for I am a very ancient man, and this seems somehow new to me."

"You know; how every one is born equal - although of course some are more equal than others - and a fair distribution of labour, and justice and all of that."

"My sweet enormousness," said Rabelais, "I created Thélème in another time and for quite other reasons. Then monks and monasteries were endemic like the plague, spreading their misery and death all around them, so I founded Thélème to answer them all and dedicated the best of my energies to showing the beauties of life here. And they are beautiful, aren't they, my

Thélèmites?"

"Oh, yes they are," said Garganette, fervently.

"Well then, I made out my case for my own time. Could I do more? If other things are wrong in your time, then you must address yourself accordingly. But first get yourself an education. Many people have contributed to this library, and if you want to see other ideas, you have only to look about you: there is a great deal to see. And now you must digest your little meal and let the meats settle in your stomach by watching my young people as they dance."

So Garganette sat awhile with Rabelais as the Thélèmites, with graceful measured tread, danced solemnly to honour their fine truths, until she grew restless and, with a fond farewell of her friend, slipped quietly away.

How Garganette Pauses Awhile For Reflection

Monsieur Rabelais was quite right: there was a tremendous amount to see in the Library land, and enlivened by her encounter with him, Garganette's curiosity was awake to every idea she met and she examined every possibility most closely.

'Oh look,' she said to herself. 'Here's the Borough of Christianity! How beautiful it is. This is what Mr Butskill talked about, and I can see it so clearly now. Here everyone really is equal, and it's all explained, how the rich should feed the poor, how everyone should love everyone else, and how God loves us all, (oh yes this is a good place), how he loved us all so much that he gave us his only son to die for love of us. What? That can't be right; I must have misunderstood,' and she looked more closely, but it was right, and she further learnt that God's son had died in torment because of the sins of mankind, and that she personally had to bear the burden of guilt for this, for she was a sinner, too, and had been from birth, due to Original Sin of which everyone was guilty. And unless she repented, she would be put to the everlasting and excruciating torture of the damned, but that if she did sincerely repent of her evil ways God would forgive her. And reading on, she discovered that if she wanted to make absolutely sure of a place with God in Heaven she was advised to turn away from the world and the love of men, loving only God's son; or perhaps submit to martyrdom, which is not such a fashionable option as it once had been, but there are still opportunities of this kind. And Garganette was furthermore astonished to learn that it didn't matter what sins she committed as long as she repented, for God is a loving God and loves a repentent sinner better than anyone. 'But this is horrible,' thought the good child, and quickly left that place.

On she went, moving from one region to the next: sometimes fighting through a dark jungle of verbiage to find only emptiness at its heart; sometimes discovering mischief and nonsense behind fine words; and again coming to some beautiful place where the sun shone bright and clear illuminating great wisdom. She was by turns amazed and delighted, troubled and amused, but always glad to be there, and as she wandered she came upon a place where the people were happy, lively and living in great peacefulness with each other and she stopped to take a closer look, sitting down carefully nearby.

"Ah," said a voice at her elbow, "I see you take an interest in Nowhere."

"I beg your pardon," said Garganette, surprised at being spoken to, having foolishly thought she'd not been seen.

"This is my place, Nowhere. My name is Morris and you may call me William."

"Thank you," said Garganette. "This is a lovely land, you have here, and the people are charming. They talk so nicely with each other, and they work so cheerfully. They are also beautiful and seem somehow unafraid. It's most unusual."

"You've noticed. Good. But you see they have nothing to fear now, since they overthrew their evil masters."

"Oh, are they French?" asked Garganette, glancing askance at the happy people, for she had recently taken a distant view of Revolution, but skirted round it in alarm.

"No, no, they're not. They're English and living safe in a new England. Do you think the English bosses were not as terrible as the French?"

"Then what happened? How did they win their freedom?"

"By violence!" a new voice cried out loudly. "In dreadful violence and carnage!"

"Oh, it's you Tolstoy, is it?" said William.

"Yes it is. Now come on, tell this notable young giantess how your people shed blood to win their grand new peace."

"Blood for blood, Leo," cried William, "to stop the country falling into barbarism. Violence only in answer to violence. You can't deny it."

"That's what you say. That's how you've written it. And from violence do you really think you can get this idyllic place? It doesn't work like that, William, and you should know it. Why, when we gave the serfs their freedom..."

"Oh very good!" answered William in contempt. "You gave men their freedom! Very noble and generous of you, Count Tolstoy, to give to men what's theirs by natural right! You can't give men their freedom: they have to take it! To fight for it! And when they wrest their freedom from the cruel oppressors, the inevitable result is this beauteous land, as I have proved."

"It certainly is very attractive," said Garganette.

"It's a dream," shouted Tolstoy, jumping up and down in fury. "A myth, a fantasy! An impossibility! It's Nowhere, look!"

And as she looked, the quaint vision of happy, carefree English men and women working together in solid harmony, faded away. Garganette blinked and turned back to the two men, now arguing fiercely, nearly coming to blows in their passionate debate on how best to be free, and while she watched, almost laughing at them, almost crying, they too began to fade, until she couldn't see them any more, couldn't tell if what she heard was shouting or the distant rumble of thunder, which as it turned out was the noise her stomach made, complaining bitterly that she was very late for tea. So she gathered up her wits, put one foot in front of the other and ran all the way home to the farm.

How Garganette Goes Into Training
For A Great Meeting

Garganette slept soundly that night and when she awoke she was so eager to discuss everything with her dear teacher, Mr Couldtry-Harder, that she rushed to school and managed to arrive in her classroom just before she left the farmhouse, an occurrence so amazing that it might have had terrible consequences if anyone had noticed, for people generally can't bear impossible things to happen, but fortunately her speed was such that the most anyone was aware of was a slight jolting, as when one almost misses the next step, or some such small non-event that causes the heart to pause and makes one feel foolish, so no one gave it a second thought. It is true that there was an abnormally large number of major hurricanes and flash floods, to say nothing of twenty tremendous earthquakes; several hundred smaller islands totally vanished; the moon bounced out of the sky briefly and the earth stopped for a very short space of time, all of which might have had something to do with Garganette's impossible action, but might have been the merest coincidence, and while scientists couldn't agree amongst themselves, the people were all of the opinion that it must have been the greenhouse effect.

"Oh sir!" cried Garganette as she burst into her classroom just before waving goodbye to her mother at the farmhouse door. "Oh, sir, sir, I've got so much to tell you!"

"Lord, Garganette," said Mr Couldtry-Harder, her teacher, "what a gale you've brought with you! Shut the door quick, before I'm blown away. Now sit down and tell me what it's all about."

Garganette told him what had happened: how she'd met the

Robin, who'd told her she was looking for something; how she'd gone in search of what ever it was; where she'd gone, the people she'd met and what they had told her; how she had felt very clear about everything at the time, but was now somewhat confused and needed his help to sort it all out and give her a definite aim and goal.

Mr Couldtry-Harder blinked.

"Well, Garganette,"he said after thinking it over."That's a huge problem you've presented me with."

"Yes, sir," said Garganette proudly.

"And I think that what you should aim for is, in fact, the truth."

"Oh, yes!" cried Garganette. "How wonderful! The truth, of course! Thank you, Mr Couldtry-Harder!"

"Not at all," said her teacher with modest pride.

"Well, sir, and can you tell me how to find the truth, please?"

"Well," said he. "It's not as simple as that. H'm. I mean, I'm not sure that I know myself. But, you know," he added hurriedly, noticing the disappointment gathering in great clouds on his pupil's face, and anxious as ever to please her, "the first thing is to get an education; your Mr Rabelais was quite right about that. There is to be a gathering of all the greatest Philosophers,Mathematicians and Scientists: all the most educated and intelligent men and women in this country, and many from the rest of the world, will be meeting at the Great Centre of Learning in a few weeks. I will personally educate you up to the highest possible standards and then you shall go and meet with them. How's that, my dear Garganette?"

"Oh, sir!" cried Garganette, greatly excited. "Thank you so much. I can hardly wait! Can we begin at once?"

So they sat down and Mr Couldtry-Harder told Garganette everything he knew, and she told him everything she knew; they investigated all the subjects under the sun and all the subjects hidden from the sun and everything else as well; they read all the books, checked all the sources, consulted the oracles, confided in the computer, so that by the time the Great Meeting was to take place, they were both bristling with facts and bursting with answers. Garganette could hardly contain her joy, for she felt that the brilliant gathering she was to attend must furnish her with the answer to the one great, huge, delightful, burning question she had decided to ask, namely: What is the truth?

How Garganette Met The Specialists

Garganette was greatly delighted at the prospect of meeting so many eminent and learned men and women, each one an expert in his chosen field, and she arrived at the Great Centre of Learning her courage high and heart aglow with the fervency of her desire to crown her knowledge with the acquisition, at last, of the truth.

"Ah, Miss," murmured an elderly man wearing blue livery, white stockings and a powdered wig, "the Ladies and Gentlemen are expecting you. Pray, follow me," and he led Garganette to a huge hall from which came a tremendous noise and inside there were more specialists than could possibly be found anywhere in one place. What a sight they made! There were specialists in:

Physics	Sociology	Demography
Metaphysics	Geology	Geography
Astrophysics	Theology	Calligraphy
Particle Physics	Biology	Historiography
Whole Physics	Neurology	Biography
Holistics	Psychology	Hagiography
Statistics	Computology	Typography
Logistics	Campanology	Oceanography
Linguistics	Astrology	Telegraphy
Mathematics	Marine Biology	Photography
Pure Mathematics	Archaeology	Iconography
Applied Mathematics	Anthropology	Cinematography
Rheumatics	Cardiology	Topography

Pneumatics	Urology	Stenography
Politics	Choreology	Spectrography
Economics	Eschatology	Pornography
Politics & Economics	Graphology	Orthography
Political Economy	Horology	Autobiography
Economical Politics	Behavioural Psych.	Autonomy
Ergonomics	Physiology	Democracy
Philosophy	Physiognomy	Plutocracy
Theosophy	Gynaecology	Theocracy
Iconoclasty	Paediology	Aristocracy
Astronomy	Philology	Meritocracy
Anatomy	Philately	Mediacracy
Gastronomy	Zoology	Mediocrity
Agronomy	Morphology	Pandocracy
Chemistry	Mineralogy	Technocracy
History	Genealogy	Bureaucracy
Tapestry	Geniality	Hypocrisy
Embroidery	Ontology	Ethnocracy
Joinery	Giantology	Ornithocracy
Carpentry	Dwarfology	Ornithography
Carpetry	Arachnology	Choreography
Artistry	Geomorphology	Monography
Surgery	Technology	Anography
Brain Surgery	Ideology	Eidography
Micro Surgery	Phenomenology	Logography
Cosmetic Surgery	Criminology	Myography
Notoriety	Anotherology	Heligraphy
Gastronomy	Pharmacology	Cyclography
Engineering	Melanchology	Ecolography
Civil Engineering	Immunology	Chronography
Civic Engineering	Meteorology	Chorography
Maintenance Eng.	Chronology	Chromography
Electrical Engineering	Musicology	Cheirography
Royal Engineering	Terpsichore	Cymography
Genetic Engineering	Calliope	Thaumatography

Social Engineering	Teleology	Haplography
Steam Engineering	Endocrinology	Hygrography
Agriculture	Ophthalmology	Olegraphy
Architecture	Methodology	Hymnography
Sculpture	Epistemology	Homography
Horticulture	Murology	Eidography
Viticulture	Epidemiology	Thermatography
Viniculture	Lymphology	Electrography
European Culture	Ornithology	Cosmography
Greek Culture	Olfactrology	Spirography
Sociologistics	Sociobiology	Gutturography
Neurolinguistics	Sphagnology	Autography
Sociometry	Sphygmology	Lithography
Trigonometry	Haematology	Spherography
Electronics	Zymology	Serigraphy
Ethics	Palaeontology	Hydrography
Phonetics	Spelaeology	Ideography
Peripatetics	Somatology	Phraseography
Diuretics	Muscology	Physiography
Magnetics	Bryology	Helicography
Histrionics	Ethnology	Zoography
Idiotics	Egyptology	Graphography
Cosmetics	Ethnology	Osteography
Corybantics	Christology	Phytogeography
Parabolics	Etymology	Seismography
Hieroglyphics	Scientology	Thalassography
Dialectics	Judology	Sphygmography
Diametrics	Judaeology	Dactylography
Obstetrics	Hellenology	Pterylography
Narcotics	Doxology	Ichthlography
Cherubics	Feminology	Thlipsography
Aviatrix	Bimbology	Lexicography

and a team of Pancryptopolychromatopseudopsychozoazymo-
comptutovirographologicians whose specialism was the care

and understanding of the great banks of computers, and in the midst of all these brilliantly learned persons was a single rabbit, which leapt about with astonishing acrobatic skill, while the scientists grabbed at it.

"Come here, you little brute," cried a Cardiologist. "Gotcha! Now see here," he shouted over the noise made by the others, "just here," and he tore at the rabbit and would have torn its heart right out but the rabbit wriggled and squirmed and managed to free itself just in time. "Damn and blast the little ...!" muttered the Cardiologist.

"Oh nonsense," yelled an eminent Urologist, clutching the rabbit out of the air as it leapt passed. "Just let me get to its kidneys and I'll show you what I mean."

"That's crap!" roared one of the women. "What you want to do is take off its head and get at its psyche. I'm a Pissologist and I know. I mean," she said, blushing, "I'm a Psychologist. You're the Pissologist," she said to the Urologist, and she burst out laughing.

"Ha ha ha! Pissologist!" everyone laughed, except the Urologist. "He he he! Pissologist!"

"What *are* you doing with that rabbit?" asked Garganette.

"Oh, she's here," they cried, while the rabbit seized its opportunity and with its remaining strength leapt into Garganette's arms, where it lay panting and exhausted.

"We're discovering the Truth, you know," said an Ophthalmologist, sincerely.

"How do you mean?" asked Garganette.

"Just give me that rabbit's eyes and I'll show you."

"Oooo!" breathed the rabbit and fainted.

"Give you its eyes?" asked Garganette. "What good are its eyes without the rest of it?"

The Ophthalmologist gave her a sincere smile, while the others gazed at her pityingly. "I'm an Ophthalmologist," he explained kindly. "I specialise in eyes. What good is the whole rabbit to me when I can learn everything I need to know just by studying its eyes?"

"But...but I'm looking for the truth," said Garganette.

"And so are we," said a wise Egyptologist. "The rabbit as such is of no use to me: embalm it and in three thousand years or so I may be able to tell you a little about it, how it lived and so on. Ah, indeed, the way to the Truth is hard and long. That's why we specialise."

"But I want to know the whole truth," said Garganette.

A great gasp came from the Giants of Intellect gathered about her, while some of the more nervous among them tittered in their surprise.

"The whole Truth! That's impossible! Unthinkable! Be reasonable, young woman! Look at that rabbit you're holding! You can't seriously expect to know everything about it! The amazing complexity of the thing! My goodness, give me air before I fall!"

"Doesn't any of you know all the truth, then?" asked Garganette.

"No!" they cried. "The Truth is too large for any one person to grasp in its entirety. No one is big enough."

"What about me," said Garganette, "aren't I big enough?"

"H'm. Ah. Well," they said. "We'll have to think about that. Come back in a year or two and we'll be able to tell you. Meanwhile, just hand over that rabbit, will you."

But this Garganette refused to do, much to their disappointment, and after thanking them most politely, she left with the rabbit secure in her arms.

"Phew!" said the rabbit. "What a load of... Well, anyway thank you for coming in time to rescue me. Much obliged, I'm sure. Mind you, that'll teach me to believe everything I read."

"What do you mean?" asked Garganette.

"Just that I read in the sits vac that they were looking for a young rabbit to help them in their researches into Life, the Truth and Everything, with good pay and conditions and free accommodation. Hah! I bet they wouldn't even have accommodated me in a coffin when they'd finished. Had me for dinner, more like, if there'd been enough left of me to cook. Well, dear young Giantess, you can put me down in this nice meadow; I've got some cousins hereabouts. I hope you find what you're looking for. And many, many thanks. You saved my life, you know."

Garganette set him down and they parted with affection, and went their separate ways. Garganette felt she had learned much that day, what with one thing and another, but still she seemed no nearer the truth. Ho hum.

How Garganette Journeyed Home

Garganette watched her Rabbit friend as he bounded away and the last she saw of him was his white fluffy tail disappearing down a burrow.

'Well,' she thought, 'I'd best be getting home myself. Now what would be the best way?' She pulled the railway timetable out of her pocket and after studying it closely for some time, decided finally that it would be better, more comfortable, and certainly quicker to walk: for what is 300 miles to a strapping young giantess? and on such a lovely day as this it would be a shame and a waste to loll about on a train. So she walked, and musing, covered many miles most pleasantly, while the gentle landscape around unfolded its beauties to her; the world was putting on its fresh spring greenery; birds were flirting; daffodils blooming; lambs leaping; everything seemed most optimistically discontented and the whole scene was bathed in the soft golden sunlight.

Garganette strode along, sidestepping towns and cities, sticking to the green and pleasant part of the land, where she began to realise that everything seemed keen and eager to recreate itself after the dull hard winter, instead of having a rest in the sun, and she had not seen this restlessness before.

She came to the town nearest her home and decided to sit awhile in the park, and there she found the people were behaving oddly too. Old persons of forty years or more, lying in the grass kissing and cuddling. Ancient men and women strolling hand in hand or sitting with their arms around each other happily. 'Well,' thought Garganette, 'what does it mean?' for this too was something she had not seen before. Then some boys came past, swaggering by a group of giggling girls, who ignored them and were chased screaming with laughter and pretended fear. 'Well,' thought Garganette, much amazed. 'What can it mean?'

Then, as the shadows began to lengthen, a solitary boy came up to her and said, "You're Garganette, aren't you?" and he sat on the grass quite close to her, pulling up stalks and chewing on them.

"Yes," she said, "and you're Gorgeo, aren't you?"

"Yes," he said and gazed hard into the distance, while Garganette thought, 'well, I've known him all my life, but I've never really seen him before. It must mean something?' She felt very interested in him suddenly and somehow excited. She wondered all sorts of things, but said nothing.

"You're ever so pretty, Garganette," said Gorgeo suddenly in a deep gruff voice.

"Oooh!" said Garganette, very surprised that he should have noticed and feeling even more interested in this clever, witty boy. "Do you think so?"

"Yes, definitely," said Gorgeo, and they had somehow edged closer together.

"I think you're pretty too, in a handsome kind of way," said Garganette, in a voice deeper than usual.

"Oh," said Gorgeo, blushing and looking sternly pleased.

"Gorgeo," said Garganette, extremely shyly and doubtful of his reaction. "Gorgeo, I hope you won't mind my asking, but there's something I really very much want to know." For some reason Gorgeo blushed, but Garganette was blushing too, and he nodded.

"Gorgeo," said Garganette very earnestly, her voice getting

deeper and softer, "would you mind, I mean I hope you don't mind, but say if you do, but can you, I mean could I, I mean will you, I mean can I," here Garganette decided to take the bull by the horns, as it were, come to the point, get to the very nub and heart of the matter and taking a deep breath, said most huskily, "can I see your whatsit, please?"

"Oh!" said Gorgeo, all of a gasp, whispering. "Oh yes, of course, certainly, here it is!"

"Oooh!" and Garganette was whispering too as she peered at it in the gathering twilight. "Its very nice, Gorgeo," she murmured pressing up close to him. "Can I touch it, please?"

"Oooh, yes," whispered Gorgeo, and she put her great fingers to it delicately and was immensely surprised to feel it swell up in her hand.

"Oh Gorgeo!" she whispered excitedly. "Isn't it lovely?"

"Ooh, yes!" whispered Gorgeo hotly.

Then at this interesting stage they were suddenly interrupted by the voice of the Park Keeper shouting, "Come on you lot! Locking up time! Off you go! I don't know, kids," and at this Garganette felt Gorgeo's whatsit disappear, and she was so upset that she almost started to cry. "Oh, Gorgeo!" she wailed. "Where has it gone? What have I done? Your lovely thingy!"

"Oh, please don't cry, Garganette," said Gorgeo, kissing her. "I'm sure it'll come back if you were to hold it again."

"Come on, you kids, out!" shouted the Park Keeper.

"Are you sure, Gorgeo?"

"Meet me tomorrow and you'll see," said he.

"See you tomorrow then, Gorgeo," said Garganette smiling again.

"Tomorrow," said Gorgeo. Then he ran away while Garganette bounded off as happy as a sky lark.

94

How Mavis Welcomes Her Daughter Home

"Oh, Garganette! There you are at last!" said Mavis, when Garganette bounced in from her travels. "Wherever have you been? What took you so long? I've been so worried! And how are you, dear? You look a bit flushed. Are you alright?"

"Oh, mummy," said Garganette. "I'm fine, really." She wanted to tell Mavis all about Gorgeo and his wonderful whatsit which had grown so enormous in her hand and had then disappeared, and how she hoped it would be there tomorrow, and how she would very much like Gorgeo to see her own thing. She would have liked to discuss this with her mother, to find out how best to go about it, and what exactly a girl should do when showing her doo-la to a boy for the first time, but somehow she didn't think Mavis would respond very well to all this, so she said nothing about the subject, but only sighed and was restless.

"Well, Garganette," said Paul, "and have you found the Truth then?"

"Oh, daddy!" said Garganette, very much surprised to think that Paul knew about her and Gorgeo.

"And what did all those clever scientists tell you, then?" asked Paul, who was reading the fat stock prices.

"Oh, well, as to them, not very much, but I have learned something," said Garganette, giggling and grinning and flopping down on the sofa and the floor, sitting first in one place and then another, rolling over onto her belly, her back, her side, not finding rest anywhere, and not looking for it, but feeling gloriously comfortable in herself all the same.

"Whatever is the matter, Garganette?" said Mavis. "Do keep still. Have you got a fever? You've caught something nasty with all those Professors and things! I knew nothing good would come of it, going off like that! And I bet you walked home instead of taking the train like I told you! I know you're big, Garganette, but you mustn't take liberties with your health. It's the most important thing you've got!"

Garganette laughed happily, but not wanting to offend her Mother's delicate Maternal Feelings turned it into a cough.

"Oh you see! Now you're coughing! You have caught something. Off to bed at once!"

"That's right," said Paul, "I want you to be up bright and early so you can help on the farm. It's very busy right now."

"Oh no!" said Mavis firmly. "She's staying in bed till she's quite better!"

"Oh no!" said Garganette, "I can't do that! I've got some very important research to do with one of the boys."

"Garganette," said Mavis, putting her foot down, "your health comes first."

"Oh, no, mummy, the truth always comes first,"said Garganette, piously, and kissing her parents goodnight, she went to bed.

And in the morning she was off trembling with excitement to pursue her studies into the very nature and fabric of the truth.

How Garganette And Gorgeo
Pursued Their Researches

Garganette was up early the next morning and presented herself at the breakfast table glowing with health and eager anticipation: so pink and healthy did she look that Mavis at once assumed her child must be very ill.

"Garganette, you're flushed," she said, "I'm sure you have a temperature. Go back to bed at once and I'll call the Doctor."

"Oh, mummy, really," said Garganette through the mammoth mound of her customary breakfast.

"No, darling, you mustn't eat, remember: feed a cold and starve a fever. Off to bed at once or you'll get seriously ill, and oh my goodness!" cried Mavis tears welling at the thought, "you might even die! Oh, Garganette! Oh, Garganette!"

But Garganette had already left the farm house and was on her way to the long meadow, where she found Gorgeo. Now, at sight of each other, the two young people were at first a little shy, but they very much wanted to continue their researches and were soon as close to each other as they had been on the previous night.

"I would very much like," said Garganette, "to reassure myself as to the well-being of your thingy: to make sure that it will grow fine and strong again as it did yesterday."

"Oh, please do," said Gorgeo, delighted, "and I would like, if I may, dear Garganette, to see your thingy. Do you think you could allow me to?"

"Oh, yes," said Garganette, delighted in her turn to help him in any way she could. "I'm sure I should like that very much."

Gorgeo was completely overwhelmed by what he saw, and gasping a little, declared he had never seen anything to equal it.

"Oh," he sighed in delighted wonderment. "How beautiful! How unusual! To think that where I have my dingle-dangle you have all these accoutrements! How charming and exquisite! May I, sweet Garganette, take a leisurely look at all you have displayed before me here, so that I might familiarise myself with the wonder of it and the special uses to which you put all this loveliness?"

To this request Garganette was extraordinarily pleased to agree, and while Gorgeo was busy investigating the fleshly charms of Garganette, she was similarly busy discovering all about him, and with expressions of mutual pleasure they continued in this delightful study all the day: kissing and cuddling rapturously from the fresh early morning, right through noon and never leaving off until the setting of the sun made it too dark to see each other. Then, at last, they parted with regret, but promising to meet again the next morning, in the same place, for they both felt instinctively that there was much left for them to learn.

"Garganette! Garganette! Where have you been?" cried Mavis at the farm house door. "I've waited for you all day and you never came home for you dinner or your tea, you bad girl! I've been so worried! Oh, my poor heart! You could have been lying dead somewhere, and I wouldn't have known! Or a wicked man might have got hold of you and hurt you!"

"Ha, ha!" laughed Garganette, happily.

"No, Garganette, you shouldn't laugh. Such things happen to innocent little children. It's time you and I had a little talk about things."

"Ha, ha, mummy," laughed Garganette, "who could hurt me?"

But Mavis kept on grumbling and complaining until Garganette, overcome by sleepiness, suddenly yawned and used up all the air in the place, creating a temporary vacuum and leaving her family for a moment without oxygen, which made them confused and drowsy and was very effective in keeping her mother quiet.

So it continued for the rest of that brief and glorious holiday: Garganette and Gorgeo met each morning and satisfied their lust for knowledge all day. Then on the last afternoon, Gorgeo said, "Sweet Garganette, tomorrow we must return to school and though we shall see each other there, we will have very little time to devote to this most exquisite course of study, but will have to do our Maths and Ologies."

"Mmm," said Garganette, kissing him agreeably.

"Because of that," went on Gorgeo, whispering huskily, "I would very much like to try one thing we have not so far done. Dear Garganette, could we not see if our thingies, yours and mine, fit together snugly, as I'm sure they should?"

"Oh, Gorgeo," whispered Garganette, "I would love to try. But one thing troubles me. I am concerned that if we do this, out of love for you I might swallow you all up, and though it would be charming to have you with me always, I should miss you very much, on the outside as it were!"

"Oh, Garganette, you are wonderful. You have voiced the very doubt that I too have had. But I'm sure we must take the risk, for I feel certain that our thingies were made for each other, and think we should definitely do it. And if you do inadvertently swallow me all up, I should be most happy to live inside you always."

So they solemnly agreed and commending themselves and each other to their happy fate they embraced, and then with great pleasure they did try and Garganette did swallow Gorgeo all up: they were both quite sure of that, and were therefore most surprised a little later to discover each other lying quite complete and separate beside each other. This they decided must be a paradox and were immeasurably gratified that the experiment had been a complete success, and nothing would content them but to do it again, immediately they had quite recovered their energies, just, you know, to make quite sure they absolutely knew the right way to go about the thing.

How Garganette Returns To School

Now it was the time to once more pick up the threads of sober life and return to school, where Mr Couldtry-Harder was waiting to find how Garganette had got on at the Great Meeting of Philosophers, Mathematicians & Scientists, and to remind her that she was to give a Speech before the whole School, to acquaint them with her Learning and be a Credit to his Educational Methods and the State School System.

Ah, but it was hard to prepare such a mammoth undertaking and she was given every help and encouragement, and allowed to study as she chose, so she spent her time writing poetry to her love and sighing, and pulling faces at the younger children who were sent to bathe her fevered brow, until at last the day of reckoning came. From early morning the hall was packed with excited, expectant children and their teachers, all of whom knew, because they had been told, that on this day, at this very hour, the fruits of Garganette's learning, the key to knowledge itself was to be given them by their great colleague.

And here verbatim is that wondrous, enlightening speech.

Garganette's Speech

Wakhtakawath having discovered the
owl lake attempts to swim across.
The owls, however, resenting this,
conspire with Ishaivishqoi, whose
twelfth wife, Wrookuvroo, Wakhtakawath
desires. Ishaivishqoi encourages
Wrookuvroo, red shank marsh harrier,
to perform the dance of the golden
oriole, after which she is transformed
into a vole which the owls devour.
The owls' revenge is complete when
Ishaivishqoi consigns Wakhtakawath
in the ever swirling fires of water,
and the regurgitated pellet of the
vole/wrookuvroo, having been fertilized
in this fire, becomes the giant
skort weed.

Here and now at this juncture, within this here-and-now, we have of course chaos, that is the nothingicity in which you find yourselves, prior to the Somethingness which you will gain from the consequential synthesis of understanding I now bring and it will be as well to bear in mind the above fable, F993701(c).

To begin then within the parameters designated it follows, is indeed axiomatic, that the function of speech and language in any psychoanalytical philosophy will be determined by praxis, which can be demonstrated almost at random, but to subvert ambiguity, a necessary concomitant to the facilitation of the acquisition of clarity, we will use the pivotal line A-B, where B is merely the oppositional correlation of A as I have proved, and will so prove again.

For it is simply a question of grasping more precisely the articulation of doctrines given.

100

And it is here, at the sensitive frontier between truth and knowledge, that the first aporia interpolates itself into the dialectic, which to deoppilate the immanenticity of the algorithm necessitates a conjunctural convergence or parallelism, as Professor Lackall has said in his usual clear and forthright style.

Can it thus be that the man of place (viz Helmholtz) could have 'no-place' in this periodicity described? I would to heaven it were so, but the Hegelian Historicity underlying - though could it not be said undermining? - the phenomenology would - and heavily underscoring - not have it so; whereas summarizing it in this way leaves the philosophical pertinence, in the last resort, to a facilitated situating of the subject - namely in the cultural schemata.

Thus it follows that the structural dynamism and ontological libidinism of supraconscious knowledge in my reflections on the 'Aha-Erlebnis' of Kohler, oppose any situational apperception directly issuing from the 'Cogito' according with the 'I' as we experience it in psychoanalysis; though should it not here be remembered - the specular image maintained in the symbolic matrix necessarily precipitated in a form prior to objectification - and formulated in a primordial dialectic of identification, that language restores to it before, and in the universal, its function as an irreducible subject?

(A great gasp went out from the audience, but Garganette was adamant).

It must be so; any lingering doubt must be dispelled by the schedules of reinforcement and cognitive markers authenticated in the connaturality implied in signifier and signified; and what wide ranging possibilities for méconnaissance where there would be those sufficiently uninformed in the presumption that belies this sort of logic!

And yet, the matter refuses to rest there, and it becomes more than ever vital to initiate the concatenation which links the signifier to the ascesis along the complementarity of the axis, much as if it were a daisy in a chain itself a daisy in a chain made up of a chain of daisies in a daisy chain.

Finally, if, as it seems, your indignation has been aroused over these facts, all your questions and justifiable fury must be apportioned fairly amongst the disseminators of hypocrisy and pseudo-philosophical obscurantism from whose emanations this dialectic in all its vacuity had been culled; or to symbolize it succinctly and accurately in the only way possible, let me just add this," and Garganette, in a gesture worthy of her ancestry, let loose a mighty fart which rent the air.

How This Speech Was Received

Well! What a triumph! The applause which greeted this speech was simply tremendous! Garganette called for questions but there were none, for after so lucid a lecture delivered in such scintillating and yet limpid language, who could possibly have any questions? And it was wonderful to all who heard her how well she had understood her subject and how well she had imparted her knowledge so that no one could escape her meaning. It is true that one of the younger children, weeping with confusion, declared that he hadn't understood anything and begged to be told it again, but they muffled his cries and bundled him out, and the poor child went on to become a poet (oh dear), and was knocked down by a bicycle on the pavement outside the sweet shop in Kentish Town Road, so he never learnt anything, did he? But Garganette was heaped with honours:BAs, MAs, MBAs by the score, PhDs, MScs, FRICs, ARCs, SKITs, SNITs - oh she had letters after her name which stretched from here to the Christmas before last; Professorships; Doctorates; lucrative lecture tours; and she was even put up for the Nobel Peace Prize but was found to have too pacific a nature. The cheering lasted for hours, the party went on for weeks, but after the noise died down, after the hubbub and hullaballoo were over, Garganette lay with her Gorgeo for a tender adieu. *He* had to stay on for his

As and then go to university, but Garganette had done with schooling and set her heart on an education.

How Garganette Goes To The City In Search Of Truth

Ah, Garganette. How far you have come: down the endless avenues and by-ways of childhood, through the intricacies of your young life, travelling in the forests of learning with patience and courage, encountering the knottiest thickets with acquisitive curiosity until now, on the threshold, nay with both feet firmly planted at the very door of dawning adulthood you stand, pausing only to savour the freshness of the coming day, poised to blaze a new path through all doubt and misconception, ready with truth and knowledge as your company to lead all humanity across the desert of ignorance to a new world of light and love and freedom.

See how she comes, magnificent youth, see her enter the city, home of greatness and learning. See how, though night has come and she is weary, her step is sure and her bearing noble. See, as under the benign, star-blazing summer sky, the street lamps light her way to an open space where, without disturbing anyone, she may lay down her sleepy head and in blissful optimistic dreams while away the hours until morning comes.

Of Specialists And Wimps

Morning did come, and as she waked, Garganette had an extraordinary and indescribable sensation. She seemed to be aware, as in a dream, of little squeaky voices making various statements, the meanings of which were difficult to grasp, such as:

"Now, this here measures 36 x 54.04 ¾ and has a cubic capacity of - are you making a note of all this?"

"But this is a fantastic opportunity to demonstrate the exact nature of the pigmentation to be found in...."

"Now look here, old man, frankly we don't have time to worry about all that, just you help me to get into the alimentary canal for observation. I've got a chart here, but I need some assistance getting down the nasal tract."

"But why don't you go the other way? There's sure to be plenty of room."

"Can't, old man, Wombworrier and Üpbüng have got a cartel operating and won't let anyone else have a look in...."

"Look, by my calculations the tensile strength which could be exerted by the operation of this...."

Then there were other voices, coming from further off and even more shrill and squeaky, which whined, "But really we don't think you should be doing this. It's a gross invasion of Garganette's civil liberties...."

Then near at hand, "These fingernails! My God these fingernails! Get some parings here while I run down to the toes to take measurements there...."

They shouted in her ears, shone lights in her eyes, blew air up her nostrils, poked and prodded, clattered and clicked, clambered and stumbled all over her until at last she was woken by one of them sticking a needle into her for blood.

"Ooh!" she yelled and opened her eyes. What an amazing sight she saw! Hundreds of little men scurrying about all over her body like a swarm of ants on the farmhouse kitchen floor. And they were all armed with theodolites, set squares, metre

sticks and slide rules; arc lamps, stethoscopes, rectoscans, hyperdermics and little bags, boxes and bottles; video cameras, microphones and Personal Computers, and they were all measuring, weighing, calculating, classifying, labelling and numbering every last little part of her.

"Ugh!" cried Garganette, naturally squeamed by the ghastly sight these little men made. "Shoo! Shoo!! Go away! Get off!"

"Now, now, Garganette," said one who happened to be investigating her ear and so could be plainly heard. "We are Specialists and we are working in the name of Science, you know; you wouldn't want to impede scientific progress, now would you, dear?"

"Yes, I would," said Garganette firmly and hooked him out. "Off you go! Off!" and she brushed them away with her hand and didn't rest until she was quite sure that every one of them had gone, for she knew you had to be very firm with ants, which while they are harmless, are most persistent.

"We'll come back!" they shouted as they ran away. "We'll get a court order, you see if we don't!"

"We told you so! We told you so!!" came another cry. Garganette looked round and saw, standing at a safe distance, a group of men who were carrying placards which read: HANDS OFF GARGANETTE and NO INVASION OF CIVIL LIBERTIES and LIBERATION NOW.

"We told them, Garganette," these men shouted smugly, in little thin voices, "we told them not to do it!"

"Grr!" said Garganette, understanding immediately how these little men would best prefer to be addressed, "and a fat lot of good you were!"

"Anytime! Anytime at all we can help you, we'll come running. Wake us up in the middle of the night! Take us from our food or our families! Interrupt us in our work or our leisure! Anytime, just call on the Wimps and we'll do anything for you. Anything! Anything! Please, Garganette, please, walk on us, sleep on us, beat us, despise us! Oh! Oh! Just anything we can do!"

"Ugh," said Garganette. "Oh very well, get me an enormous breakfast at once!"

"Yes yes," sighed the Wimps in a severe ecstasy, and hurried away to do her bidding before she changed her mind.

After she had eaten enough to feed two large standing armies for a week, and all most delicious food, Garganette was about to thank them most kindly, but she remembered in time to say ungraciously, "Call that a meal?" for to be polite to a Wimp would cause him terrible distress.

"Oh, Garganette!" they cried. "What else do you need? Tell us, please tell us! We'll get it for you, please, please!!" and they clamoured humbly around her.

"Go away, now. Leave me," she commanded. "I must look for the truth," then forgetting herself she let the benison of her golden smile break upon them. Instantly eighteen fainted, two nearly died, six took holy orders, and the rest scattered to the four winds, all in a state of most horrible shock.

'Oh dear,' thought Garganette, 'I must be more careful.'

Then she heard a little voice saying her name and she peered down to find one solitary Wimp looking up at her.

"Well," she said trying to be stern, "what do you want, Wimp?"

"I'm not really a Wimp, please Garganette," he said bashfully but with a little pride showing at the edges. "I just wondered if you don't mind, whether you'd care to come with me and allow me to introduce you to the Wimmin, please."

"The Wimmin, eh? Yes I've heard of them vaguely. That's not a bad idea. Lead on, wotsyourname, lead on."

"Claude, please," said the Wimplet. "It's a bit early for the Wimmin, as they generally don't like to come out before dark, but I have some influence with them and think I can persuade them to see you."

"Then lead on little Claude, and I will follow you," said Garganette.

To The Wimmin

Their way took them through the magnificent city: London, home for so long of greatness. Its towering buildings, all of most exquisite design, and broad avenues bustling with every kind of activity. The artists, philosophers and poets honoured on every corner. Greatness and Goodness evident in every face. Ah, wonderful, wonderful to see! And how clean the streets are, how generous and noble the people, what wonderful courtesy they display one to the other as they smile with friendly joy; how good the honest motorists are to pedestrians; with what tenacity the cyclists stick to the roads, never dreaming of endangering the lives of innocent little children on the pavements, as happens, we believe, in less glorious places. Oh, happy, happy Garganette, to be at once welcomed to the hearts of such a good-natured, witty, sparkling, kind and glamorous people as this. How they nodded and waved to her, and smiled to see her there, until at length Claude slipped away from the busy streets and they came into a strange, deserted, gloomy place where the sun had not shone in for centuries, and here Claude knelt on the cracked and broken pavement and whispered to the ground, "Oh Wimmin, dear Wimmin, come out please. I've brought Garganette to see you."

There came then, an eerie, hollow moaning, and slowly as she watched amazed, Garganette saw a paving stone lifting and at last there came in view a ghastly face, yellowed, melancholy, streaked and grim and this apparition spoke to her saying, "Welcome, sister, you must come down and join us here."

"Well, you know," said Garganette reasonably, "I can't possibly do that."

"Aaah," said the face, and disappeared again. The moaning increased and was added to by a wailing, a dreadful, drear, delinquent dirge, which swelled and fell and surged again until the head reappeared and said, "Then we must rise to meet you," and up from the ground, out from under the paving stones, from all around came the Wimmin, dozens, scores, hundreds, and more until Garganette was quite surrounded by a great throng and multitude of grey, gaunt Wimmin.

'Goodness,' thought Garganette to herself in the privacy of her own head. 'Goodness. Goodness, goodness, goodness, goodness.'

"Aaaah, sister you have come at last to join us," said the Wimmin. "Are you surprised to find so many of us here?"

"Well, frankly yes," said Garganette, "astonished. But tell me please, what is this Claude has brought me to, I mean do you live here, underground? And why?"

"Long, long ago we were the Law and all men answered to us. They did their duty and respected us, and though we were firm we were just. Then a young man of noble birth and splendid education did that most foul of crimes and in disguise and underhandedly murdered his mother."

"Ai! Ai!" shrieked the Wimmin in dreadful incantation.

"Ai Ai, indeed," resumed the first. "His mother, who had borne him, given him her breast to suck, nurtured him. This bloody deed was done, and faithful Aeschylus has well recorded all. It fell to us to take revenge: it was our duty and our right. We pursued the criminal to execute the Law on him, expecting blood for blood. But another, newer law was coming in the land and each time we came near to him, we found him protected by this law and could not get our hands on him."

"Oh! Oh!" wailed the Wimmin, "we could not get our hands on him!"

"Until at last we followed him to the greatest City of all, where he had gone for sanctuary to the court and there we demanded that in justice he be handed over to us that rightful vengeance be enacted soon."

"Justice! Justice!" shrilled the Wimmin so eagerly that Claude clung to Garganette's ankle for protection and even Garganette quailed almost for a moment.

"And did you get your justice?" she enquired.

"Aaaaargh!" screamed the speaker.

"Aaaargh! Aaaargh! Aaargh!" stormed the Wimmin.

"No we did not! The wretched coward was let free! And worse, much worse, it was decreed that henceforth the female should be merely the field, ripe for the male to sow his seed. And worse than this, the worst of all, the Goddess, mark you the Goddess who had laid down this statute also said that we, the Wimmin, should no more have custody in Law of miscreants and vile perpetrators of such savage ills. Aaaargh!" she ended on a fearsome terrible note.

"Goodness," said Garganette, "what did you do?"

"The Goddess said we must live underground and be content with the honour and the worship that men do to our great power, and we agreed, for it is right that we should be respected. It's all we ask. But now," she stormed, "the men don't care! They don't worship us any more! They don't take any notice of us, and it's not fair! It is against the Law!"

"But that was a very long time ago," said Garganette, "surely things are better now?"

Then the Wimmin all started shouting different things:

"Better! It's worse now!"

"We're not allowed to be intelligent or ambitious! We have to be decorative, adorable and dependent on our husbands!"

"I want something more than my husband, my children, my home! I want something which makes me feel I exist! That would be better!"

"In this present society and in most of the societies we know about, most men despise all women and most women despise most women as well, and that includes themselves. A woman's identity is formed in fact in ways which are almost a prescription for schizophrenia. The conditioning processes of society, advertisements, magazine stories and articles, films, novels, TV and the expectations of people around her insist that she needn't bother to be a person!"

"Wimmin should be political lesbians, and our definition of a political lesbian is a woman-identified woman who does not fuck men!"

"All men are violent!"

"All men violently oppress all women!"

"Wimmin shouldn't fuck men, they should fuck Wimmin!"

"Revenge! Revenge! We want revenge! For centuries of neglect and ill-usage! For all the injustice! Revenge! For the poverty! Revenge! For the rape! Revenge! For the humiliation! Revenge! For the pain! Revenge!"

"Let the Wimmin Revolt!"

"Let the Wimmin Rise Up!"

"Let the Wimmin Fight On!"

"Wimmin Unite!"

"Men Watch Out!"

"Oh that's good. That's very good! Wimmin Unite, Men Watch Out! Ha ha ha ha! WIMMIN UNITE! MEN WATCH OUT!! Ho ho ho ho! Isn't it lovely? Let's have a party!" and the Wimmin settled down to make a wonderful feast.

"Garganette," they said, "you shall be our guest at this feast. You have inspired us and we are grateful for your support."

Now you can imagine, gentle reader, how pleased Garganette was to see the dainty dishes spread before her, as it was late on into the evening and she was very hungry, so she ate with a light heart until her stomach was full and then she thanked them for their kindness.

"Dear Wimmin," she said, "you are most charming to have fed me so well, and I would like to assure you of my appreciation by speaking to you, and though I am young in years and you have millennia behind you, I hope you will listen to me, for I am sure with the certainty of instinct and experience that what I have to say is good."

"Garganette," said the Wimmin, "speak on, we'll gladly hear you."

"Well," said Garganette, firmly but kindly, "I think you should come out into the light."

110

"What!!!"

"Yes. Now you said you would listen. Please believe that I understand what you say and what you've suffered. Why, I've only been in the city one day and already I've met two kinds of dreadful men, the Specialists and the Wimps, but even though they are unspeakable and Weedy, they mean no harm."

"!!!"

"And really this is only two sorts of men. There are millions and millions of others, kind and generous men, who are good humoured and fun. And why should you let an ancient quarrel be the cause of depriving you of light and health? Think of all you're missing living down in the dank and smelly dark. And you know, you don't look - er how can I say - well - yes! you don't look very well after being cooped up down there all these years. And what do you do for love and sex without having lovely men?"

But this was too much for the Wimmin.

"Aaaaaaaaargh! Aaaaaaaaaaaaaargh!" they screamed and staggered stumbling to their underground home.

'Well, well,' thought Garganette. 'What did I say?' and she turned away, thinking in the dark and silence she was quite alone.

"Excuse us, Garganette," said a small group of Wimmin she had overlooked. "We're interested in what you have to say. Can we join you, please? We're not really Wimmin, you know."

"Of course you can," said Garganette, pleased to have them with her.

They went back to the park, and found splendid quarters had been arranged for her by Claude, who had regrouped the Wimps, longing as they were to do her service.

Garganette settled down happily for the night with a kind thought for those who had so helped her.

"And where will you sleep, little Claude?" she asked, patting him kindly in an intimate place for his encouragement.

"Oooh, Garganette," he squirmed. "You make me feel quite

strange when you do that."

"I'll give you my fine handkerchief for a cover. Would you like to curl up on my pillow?"

"Oh no, please, Garganette," he said with fervent modesty, and taking her handkerchief gratefully curled up at her feet.

How Garganette Made The Acquaintance Of Other People

Thus Garganette spent the night recouping her optimism after the losses of the day, and turned them into gains. When she awoke she yawned such an enormous yawn that the sun blinked in surprise. Then she stretched herself and reached so high she nudged him back on course. Then she looked around to find the faithful Wimps had prepared her breakfast, which she ate with gusto, while the Wimmin introduced themselves.

"I'm Peg, this is Meg, that's Rosy and Posy, and Betty, Eliza and Bess. We have been thinking of what you might like to do today: some of the Wimps want you to visit Leninton Spa, famed for its Waters, Red with the Blood of the Murdered Proletariat, but we think you'd prefer to meet some Blacks, for we were thinking that as you've lived so long in the countryside you won't know any of these people who can perhaps teach you many things, for we know you are a Searcher after Truth.

"Oh yes, the Blacks," said Garganette. "That's a splendid thought."

She was delighted by the prospect of visiting the black people in their home on the south side of the city. 'How like them,' she mused, 'to choose to live nearer the sun. Of course, I know it's symbolic, but it is a gesture all the same, a step nearer their sunny origins,' and her head filled with sunshine and tropical jungles with their unusual scents and sounds, she travelled south with Claude the Wimp and the young Wimmin, until she reached the abode of the Black Man in London, and was much disappointed to find his home just like any other area of the vast and sprawling Metropolis. But she laughed at her foolishness and greeted her new friends, whom she felt sure would help her in her search for truth, with a broad and shining smile upon her face.

"Oh Garganette," they cried. "Do not laugh at our suffering."

"Indeed no," she replied, "I would never do such a thing. But why are you suffering?"

"We are enslaved!" they cried.

"No!" she said, shocked to hear it.

"Yes, yes! Can't you see our chains?"

"No," she said, "I can't."

"We will open your eyes. Let us tell you how we come to be shackled. Long ago the wicked slavers came to Afrika and stole us from our glorious past to sell us for labour as if we had been beasts. Some say that our ancient Tribal Chiefs sold us for money; some say that our mothers sold us, but these are lies! LIES!"

"Ah, yes, of course," said Garganette.

"For long years we laboured so under the cruel lash of the master's whip. We sang as we toiled, lifted up our hearts and prayed to the God of our Enemy, for so long had we been kept in ignorance that we knew no other god and all our glorious Heritage had been left in Afrika."

"Afrika, Oh Afrika, Oh see how we weep for Thee!"

"The conquerors took our Land from us; we had no home; we were scattered across the earth and had no liberty. We were innocent and, as we had been taught to be, we were as little children. But at last we were no longer slaves and the White man invited us to his land. 'Come,' he said. 'Come to the home of Democracy. Live with us in England, the greatest land on earth. Be our Brothers and Sisters, for all men now are free.' But he LIED! He LIED!!"

"Oh, dear," said Garganette.

"We came, our innocent hearts lifted up to thank God for his generosity. Gladly we came to work for Democracy. To live in the land of Freedom. We were told we were free but found ourselves enslaved in factories, on buses and on trains, doing the jobs that the White man would not touch, for he is proud, proud. And we came, left our bright, glittering, sun-drenched, happy island homes, left the lands of song, of plenty and of harmony, left our Paradise on Earth, and came here to this, the best land in the World? Ah it is pitiful; we were robbed of our homes, cheated of our freedom. Our pride is again trampled in this foreign dust of England. Oh Afrika, our hearts are there with you! Our souls are yours! Claim us Afrika, for we are yours!" and they wailed in a melancholy chant so that Garganette was most upset.

"Oh, dear," she said, "I am so sorry for you."

"We don't want your pity! What good is that to us? Hear the rattle of our chains! Can you hear them?"

"Well, no," said Garganette, "I'm afraid I can't."

"See how we are shackled, imprisoned, despised! Here in this land we will never be free."

"Well," said Garganette, much troubled on their behalf, "what can be done? Wait!" she cried. "I've just had an idea. May I use your phone?"

"May I speak to Mr Million-Billion-Zillion Moneybags Junior the Third, please," was all they heard her say, for she stood up at that point and her voice was lost in the clouds, but they buzzed with excitement and wondered what she might be doing. But when she had finished her conversation, she didn't wait to answer their questions, but only said to them, "Hang on a minute. I won't be long," and she disappeared with a leap and a bound, which left them all gasping and clutching at their heads in amazement and no sooner had they got their breath back from this surprise than she returned.

"Its all fixed!" she cried. "You needn't worry anymore. You can go home!"

"What?" they cried.

114

"Yes. Isn't it wonderful. Mr M-B-Z Moneybags Jr III has bought several thousand million square units of the most beautiful land, and I've just been to see it."

"Well?" they cried.

"Oh, yes. I can swear there never was anything so beautiful. There's jungle, savannah and plains. There's elephant, antelope, zebras and lions. All sorts. Lush pastures, great lakes and rivers. Its so beautiful. But listen, guess what? It's in Africa, and best of all, it's yours!"

"What?" they cried. "Live in Africa?"

"Yes, I've fixed it so that you can all go and live there as soon as ever you like. Isn't it wonderful?" and she was so happy she would have danced but she was afraid of treading on people in the confined space.

"NO!" they yelled. "Absolutely not!"

"What?" she said.

"Garganette, really," they said, greatly offended.

"But I thought it would solve all your problems and make you happy to have a home in Africa."

"Garganette, please. Don't be so naive. Really! We have to stand and be proud. Listen, if you are so keen on the Truth and want to Learn come with us to the Great Gathering and you can see for yourself."

And as truth was the very thing Garganette was after, and as learning is the way to truth, she went with them gladly enough to the Great Gathering, and she hoped to learn a lot of truth, which she needed to dispel a certain confusion she felt growing up within her.

At The Great Gathering

It was impossible to miss the hall where the Great Gathering was to be held if you were looking for it, for everywhere there were bright red and yellow posters with green arrows, and a huge crowd of people, among whom were many Yooves, that is young men of both sexes and all races, was waiting for the doors to open.

Garganette sat at the back so that smaller persons would have a clear view of the stage. She surveyed the crowd until a large man stepped on to the stage and all the people cheered.

"Megabuck! Megabuck! Rankin, man, Rankin!" they cried.

Megabuck opened his mouth and it was so enormous that even Garganette was surprised and the people stopped cheering.

"Waaaa!" cried Megabuck from the back of his throat. "What do we want?"

"Liberation now!" cried the people.

"How shall we get it?"

"Smash the Oppressors!"

"Kill the Fascist Pigs!"

"Destroy the old, corrupt, violent order!"

"Good! Good!" cried Megabuck. "You've learnt your lessons well! And today we have with us Suckfizzle who will speak later, and first of all, specially flown in to greet us, is our famous brother, Franz Fanon! Welcome, brother, welcome!"

The people cheered wildly. Then Fanon spoke and they listened very respectfully.

"Irrepressible violence is man recreating himself," he said and the people applauded fervently. "I will quote to you from the great James Forman who wrote in his Manifesto, 'There are reparations due to us as people who have been exploited and degraded, brutalized, killed and persecuted...'"

"Yoh!" cried the people.

"'It follows from the laws of revolution that the most oppressed will make the revolution, whose ultimate goal is that we must assume leadership, total control...inside of the United States of everything that exists. The time has passed when we are second in command and the white boy stands on top. In order to achieve this reversal, it will be necessary to use whatever means necessary, including the use of force and power of the gun to bring down the colonizer.'"

"Hurray! Hurray!" cried the crowd.

"That's what James Forman the black power leader wrote. I say that it is through mad fury that the wretched of the earth can become men!" and Fanon finished his speech amid the wild cheers of the crowd. Then Megabuck embraced him and Fanon left.

"He has to catch a plane to carry his wonderful message of liberation to other oppressed peoples," explained Megabuck, "but he has left with us his great spirit of revolt. Do not weep, my people, for now we have Suckfizzle to speak to us."

Suckfizzle then came onto the stage. He was the greyest man that Garganette had ever seen, and very tall and thin.

"Dear people you are oppressed," he whined, "humiliated and deprived by the miserable white middle classes. But not all white people hate you: I do not and look, we have Garganette here with us, and whatever cause she takes up will benefit enormously. And there are poor and oppressed among the whites too, the Wimmin, the Workers and particularly the Young, who are exploited in their schools where they are taught lies by the viciousness of a system that impels them to believe that the inglorious past of England was glorious; and then they are oppressed by the Capitalists as cheap labour and are forced to sweat for their bread.

"And it is to the Youth of this country that I speak, all Youth, Black and White: Rise Up! Revolt! Destroy the Racist Rule of the Capitalists! Smash them! Bash them! Blow them up!" Suckfizzle paused and there was a deathly hush in the hall, "and then," he continued, "we will build a New World of Peace and Harmony, where we are all Brothers and everybody loves each other. And

117

if anyone raises a hand against our New World we will smash him! And if anyone doesn't like that we'll smash him, too! For anyone who is not with us is against us! And anyone who doesn't want to live in our Peace and Harmony with us, is an Enemy and deserves to Die! This must be our way and we will win - in the past Leaders of the Revolution have been weak, WE WILL BE STRONG!!"

"Hurray! Hurray! Rankin! Rankin!" the people roared and applauded until their throats were hoarse and their hands were stinging, then they stamped their feet to properly express their approval. Suckfizzle and Megabuck embraced each other, and it seemed that they were weeping, so overcome were they by the strength of their reception.

Megabuck, still with one arm around his friend, then spoke in a voice choking with emotion, "My friends, my good brothers and sisters. You have heard what our dear Suckfizzle has said. Remember his words and prepare to Lead the Great Revolution. Go out into the streets and smash the Oppressors. But before you go I must ask you now for contributions. The Revolution needs your financial support as well as your spiritual and physical support, and so do my estates in Jamaica, for since the Wicked Fascists have charge capped us we can no longer get the financing we need for the upkeep of our Island Homes. So give generously."

The people dug deep into their wallets and Garganette was impressed by the largeness of the notes they contributed. The strange sensations of confusion which she had hoped the Great Gathering would dispel, had grown stronger and she felt even less comfortable than she had, but like the true scholar she was, she believed that if one or two issues were cleared up, one or two questions answered, she would instantly feel better. So she stood up, but rather too quickly and forgetting that she was in a confined space bumped her head on the ceiling causing her even greater sensations of dizziness than she had felt before, but she shook her head to clear it, and asked her question all the same.

118

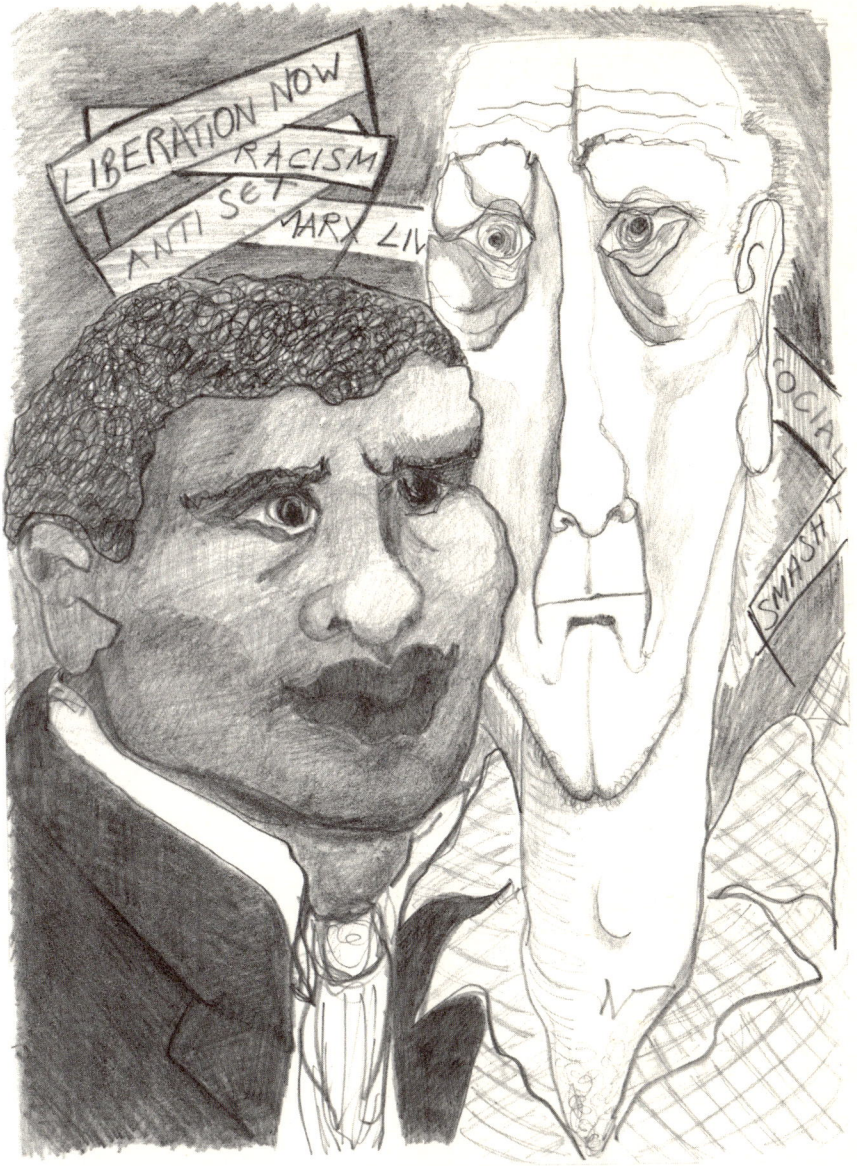

"Megabuck," she said, "thank you so much for the stimulating and interesting meeting we have just had, but there are one or two question which I would like to put to you."

"Go ahead, Garganette, go ahead," said Megabuck with a generous sweep of his outstretched arms.

"What do you intend to do after the revolution?" she said.

"Wooman, wooman," intoned Megabuck, "do not ask questions which a little child in his nursery could answer, and which no little child would need to ask. Tell her what we do after the Revolution!" he said to the crowd.

"After the Revolution? After the Revolution? That takes care of itself!"

"We all live in Peace and Harmony!"

"It's the Revolution that's the important thing!"

"Make the Revolution first and then worry about what we'll do!"

"We haven't got time to waste on these irrelevant details! Smash the Fascists!"

"Tear up their so-called civilization!"

"Tear down the Walls of the Prison!"

"Tear out the hearts of those who Oppose Us!"

"Break out in Mass Revolt!"

"Let the Wretched of the Earth be Men!"

"Don't ask stupid questions,Garganette, when you could be out doing great work for the Revolution!"

"Smash them with your big feet!"

"Crush them in your great hands!"

"Bash them with your huge fists!"

"Baash them!"

"Baaash them!"

"Baaaa!"

"Baaaaa!"

"Baaaaaa!"

Now, it may have been the knock Garganette received on her head, or it may have been the effect of all these slogans, which seemed to be buzzing around her head like a swarm of dreadful blue bottle flies, but whichever and whatever it was she suddenly felt terribly sick and not wanting to vomit on the dear people for fear of smothering them, she quickly left saying, politely, "Do excuse me," while they continued to shout and stamp and baaa and send their blue bottle slogans up into the air after her.

How Garganette Went Down The Market

To feel unwell was such an unusual event in Garganette's life that it was hard for her to know what to do, but instinct informed her she must have fresh air as soon as possible, and once outside she leaned on the building breathing in deeply, as eagerly as if she had discovered a source of cold, fresh water in a drought. Then, feeling a little better she began to look around her.

Now it happened that there was a market in the street with jolly stall-holders crying their wares:

"Cheap meat! Best cuts! Fresh wrapped in plastic for hygiene!" and there was the meat in plastic wrapping sweltering under the July sun.

"Rotten fruit! Old veg! Why buy fresh when this is just as good!"

"Toys! Toys! Straight from the factory already broken so the kiddies can't damage them!"

"Stinking fish!"

"Lovely drugs! Change your whole outlook on life!"

"Double unglazed glazing!"

Bolts of cloth that had got the moth, nylon parading as silk; electrical goods off the back of a lorry; second hand cloths whose smell told the stories of other bodies they had covered. Everything cheap! Everything broken, rotten or soiled!

Young women and old ramming each other with push carts and trolleys; children weeping or wild; huge swelling carrier bags stuffed with bargains, clutched by their owners grimly determined to save.

In and out of the stalls, keeping close to the ground were the down and outs, retrieving fallen vegetables and fruit, waving bottles, sunk down in heaps, vomitting, cursing, brawling; and beggars whining their demands.

"Arms! Oh, give arms!" cried one to Garganette as she went by, "Hand grenades, kalashnikovs, inter-continental ballistic missiles! Any little ting that you have!"

And he began to sing this sentimental ballad:

"Give arms, oh give arms to the Provos,
The boldest boys you've ever seen!
We won't shoot your babies, except by mistake,
But what you don't give us we will just take,
So give arms to the brave boys in Green
Oh give arms to the brave IRA!"

Then as she walked on she was met by two men with big beards and fierce dark faces. They wore long skirts and strange head gear and they danced in front of her crying their song:

"I'm a mad, mad Mullah!
He's an awful Ayatollah!
Give us a Rouble
Or gives us a Dollar!

Oh you naughty Garganette
Why on earth do you stare?
You mustn't laugh at us
'Cos it's just not Fair!
Watch out! Watch out! We're coming to get you!"

Stepping carefully over these she was next confronted by an old, sad man who seemed oddly similar.

121

"Are you also a Mullah, sir, or an Ayatollah?" she enquired.

"Ach, lieber Gott!" he replied in some considerable shock. "No! No! I am of the chosen people. One of the unfortunate children of Israel. You, young woman, should be ashamed to wander the streets with your arms and legs so brazenly naked before the sight of God! Go and repent of your evil ways to the Lord!" and he wandered away, muttering into his beard.

But here was another man in a long dress, a black gown reaching to the ground and, poor man, he had an injury, for round his neck was a white bandage. This time Garganette asked no questions, and the man smiled upon her and waved his hand up, then down, to his left and the right, and said, "God bless you, my child!"

And after the priest's blessing came the gipsy's curse and Garganette was unsure of the difference or how to react to any of this, but they all clamoured round her and put out their hands to her, palms up, and all entreated her to give generously.

Until at length she came to the end of the market, her head more filled with confusion than ever, and it seemed that even her vagina was no longer sure of its own sweet self.

"Ah, good afternoon! good afternoon!" said a bustling little man. "You've just come from the Great Gathering, haven't you? You're very lucky, you know. I wanted to go but they wouldn't let me in."

"Oh?" said Garganette. "Why did you want to go? Are you also searching for the truth?"

"Well of course I am," he replied, "I'm a Scientist, you know. A Psychologist. See, here's my clipboard. Now, I wonder if you'd just answer one or two questions for me. Not that I expect you'll be able to tell me anything I don't already know, but I would like to confirm my researches. Now, how did they seem to you at the gathering?"

"Well," said Garganette, thinking carefully. "They seemed to think that they were oppressed."

"Indeed! Indeed! It's as I thought!"

"And they seemed very excited, too," she added.

"Yes, yes! Statistics show that the incidence of hysterical schizophrenia is ten times as great in blacks as in whites. It's all been proved on the computer!"

"Is there anything that can be done about it?" asked Garganette who was deeply concerned.

"No, no! It's genetic. Mind you, with the advances in genetic engineering, we Scientists may soon be able to make the necessary selections and breed it out of them! Interesting thought that. Yes, we could breed it out of them, and breed into them a desire to be slaves again! Wonderful! What do you think?"

"Uk!" said Garganette, and in her haste to get away quite forgot to say goodbye.

How Garganette Went To See A Dear Friend

Then suddenly, Garganette had one brilliant thought in her head, and she knew that she must see her dear friend, Mr G Porgie, at once or sooner, for though no one else might be able to make any sense of it all, and though even Garganette herself was, to put it plainly, discouraged, fogged and mystified, it was perfectly true that Mr G Porgie would understand everything and instantly know what to do about it.

She looked around her and recognising the correct direction gave one mighty bound and in seconds was knocking at his door.

"Oh, Georgie Porgie," she cried, taking him in her arms. "Oh, you can't imagine the things I've seen and heard! Listen, listen while I tell you all about it, and see if you can believe what's going on!" Then she told him all that she had witnessed in the two short days she had been in London: the Specialists and the Wimps; the Wimmin; the Blacks and the Great Gathering; the Market and the Man with the Clipboard. Mr Porgie sat on her shoulder and listened attentively to everything, smiling, nodding, sometimes laughing, always understanding, then when she had finished, he leaned nearer to her and speaking quietly, for there was no need to shout, in a few short sentences told her the answers to the immense riddles she had set him.

Now, it is unfortunate for us that he spoke so quietly, for we couldn't hear what he said, her shoulder being so far out of our range of hearing, but Garganette heard and was delighted by what he said and they fell into each other's arms and he slipped from her arms into Garganette's own personal pool for a lovely, long, swim, which so refreshed them both that they felt there could never have been anything wrong in the world.

"And that," said Mr Porgie, "is the truth!"

"You see, darling," he told her while they were having their coffee, "you cannot know the truth until you encounter the confusions and have experienced the weight of untruth which burdens humanity."

"Oh, Georgie Porgie, you're wonderful!" said Garganette happily. "I understand it all now."

"Ha! Ha!" Mr Porgie laughed affectionately. "If you think you've seen everything, let me tell you, you ain't seen nothing yet! Take the road to the right and you'll see things there to make your hair stand on end!"

"Alright," said Garganette, who welcomed the challenge to encounter more aspects of the truth. "Thank you, Mr Porgie! Bye bye!"

And they parted happily with many touching tokens of mutual affection.

How Garganette Continues On Her Voyage
In Search Of Truth

Refreshed, invigorated and heartened by her meeting with Mr Porgie, Garganette set off down the road to the right. She had not gone far when the road divided into several streets and she had to make a choice. While she paused and tried to see which would be the best and most instructive course to follow, she got into conversation with a man who addressed her thus:

"Hi, kid! I'm Earnest Goodman, how do you do. Can't you decide which road is most right? Its a tricky one. Now, it seems to me, judging by the direction you're coming from, that you've just been visiting with the Left. Am I right or am I right? I knew it!" he cried triumphantly when she nodded. "And what do you think of them? You know, I've long believed that Socialism addresses itself to the imagination, the spirit, mankind's lust for drama. They put on a good show, sharing the Roman emperor's insight that what the public really needs is bread and circuses. It may be one of the longest playing three-hankie soap operas in history, compassion and sweetness struggling against greed and brute force, good against evil. They know how to dramatise and create stirring myths of heinous scoundrels. Democratic capitalism simply does not stir the human heart or appease its longings. So where are the soothers of the troubled masses in our type of society? I often ask myself where the Bolshie brain-mulch originated together with all the collectivist twaddle? Where do the fuzzy-minded one-worlders and the bleeding-heart bed wetters come from? In the academy, under the cloak of the critical approach, theoreticians fabricate to their hearts' content without being in any way accountable. So we get peace studies, black studies, women's studies and other such pap. Today one should look carefully again at the French Revolution because that is where much of that nonsense began with thought police, street justice and totalitarian terror, the flight from reason." He paused. "You know, kid," he went on as Garganette tried to get her breath back, "I'd like to continue this conversation with you. It's not often one meets anyone as intelligent as you are. If you ever feel like pursuing your education across the pond, you look me up and you'll be sure of a great welcome. Well now, it's time I was on my way. So long, Garganette, take care now," and raising his hat most politely he left her.

How Garganette Does Not Meet Any Yuppies

Now, Garganette had not seen any Yuppies, which she seriously wished to do, for she had heard that they were well advanced on the road to the right and were also well able to make money, a strange science of which she would have liked to know more; and though she let it be known that she wanted to meet with them, none were in any way visible or apparent.

One morning Claude the Wimp came running to her with a small parcel containing a Cellular Phone which immediately it was unwrapped rang and a voice cried: "Hey yah Gargie babe! Hear you've been looking for us? Wicked, yah! We'll have to arrange a meet! Meanwhile, buy softs, longs and shorts, but sell futures, akay? Get ya later, yah!"

Goodness, thought Garganette, thumbing through the dictionary, but all she could definitely understand was that the Yuppies had finally contacted her.

The phone rang. "Hey, Gargie yah darl, its me babe," said another completely strange voice, "how's your Electronic Data Manager Back-up System? Its a Bull market as regards coffee, but definitely Bearish as regards gold. Stay well, yah!"

Goodness, thought Garganette, I'd better write this down.

The phone rang. "Bimbo, baby hey darl. Buy cocoa, tin, tobacco, zinc; sell nothing! We'll be faxing you a PC and get you fixed up with a WS. Be lucky!"

Goodness, thought Garganette, what does it all mean? I must see these people, but where can I find them?

The phone rang. "Hey Gargie baybie..."

"Listen," said Garganette quickly, "you said something about us meeting up..."

"No, no, babe, not me!"

"Well, whoever. So how about it?"

"Well, yah hey akay. Soon, yah? Meanwhile buy dollars, Deutsch marks, Dutch crowns, French francs, Welsh Wales, but hurry, hurry, hurry!"

Garganette sent the Wimps out with a shopping list.

The phone rang: it never stopped. The voices began to complain, "Hey Gargie like babe, you're using your phone, great, wicked, but like it's important to keep the lines clear for um communication. Ya got to communicate, Bimbo baby, to be in a position of hearing and telling like, yah? I'll express you an emergency line or so for emergencies. Akay right. Hey yah and I'll fax you the details on the gilts, yah. Catch you soon."

In no time at all Garganette had banks of brilliantly coloured cellular phones growing up around her like spring flowers on the slopes of a Swiss alp, but they did not nod their pretty heads in the alpine breezes, just rang throughout the day and night as anxious Yups came on line with the latest information.

"We've definite indications of Asset Stripping..."

"Coo!"

"And probable news of Insider Dealing. So just keep an eye on Claude and those Wimmin."

"Cor!"

"An amicable settlement is expected in the recent Courtship..."

"Aah!"

"And yes, no, wait, yes! There have been several Hostile Bids!"

"No!"

"There have been recriminations on both sides and there are signs of an imminent Takeover Battle!"

"This is serious," said Garganette, "we must prepare to defend ourselves!"

"It's okay, they've agreed to talks."

"Thank God!"

"The talks are off... They're on... They're off... Wait! Gargie, baby hey sweet: its a TRADE WAR!!!"

"WAR!" cried Garganette. "This is a disaster. We are entirely unprepared. But courage, we will stand firm and face the invader; I will lead you in the fight!"

"We don't want to fight; we want to profit. If we tread carefully and deal judiciously we can make a fine fat killing at a very modest capital outlay. Bloodshed we don't need! Think about it, Gargie, akay? Ciao!"

Garganette thought about it. She thought she would like to see these Yuppies, to sit them on her knee and fondle them so that she could know who they were and be better able to do business with them, but in all the time they had been associated she had never yet touched, tasted or smelled a Yuppie for herself and we cannot therefore give a first hand description of them, and though we heard they were smooth to the touch, sweet to the smell and slightly tart in flavour, we must and do emphasise the hearsay nature of this evidence and could not at this time guarantee its veracity.

How The Yuppies Organised A Party

The phone rang. Garganette picked it up and said, "I am not used to this. I find it most peculiar that all I know of any of you is your voice coming distorted through the line. I can't always tell whether I'm talking to a man or a woman. I have the oddest notion that each one of you is trapped somewhere in a cellular phone, imprisoned as it were by the machine, for some misdemeanour or irreverence to it, held captive in isolation without the solace of a kindly human hand or eye to comfort you. I feel a curious sensation of loneliness when I am talking to you on the phone. Please come and see me to reassure me that you are free, fit and in good health, and rid me of these melancholic doubts."

128

"Oooh surreal! But hey! Gargie babe, never mind that now! We done it! We done it! If this war goes on we'll all be trillionaires! We never could a done it without you babe!"

All the phones rang.

"Gargie, darl, we gotta party! We gotta have one big party! We thought your place, Garg! Where d'ya live! In the Park?! Droll, darl! In the Park! We'll Party in the Park! We'll fill the lake with lovely Poo! Swimming in the drink! Bubbles up your nose and ET CETERA!!"

The phones began yelling plans at each other.

"We'll hang Wizzy Wiz screens and VGAs and Custardapple Graphics on the trees for decorations! Akay, pretty, yah?"

"And we'll build a great big mountain with our lovely new Dosh and fix up a Relational Data Base for Jollying in!"

"Akay, akay! And we'll get F & M & S to do a spot of Nosh for us and... Hey babies, what is with this line, hey? The Drive's gone all Wormy on me!"

"Dross and Drong! Someone's Hacking in!"

"No! In the Wimp Environment?!"

"Eeek! Better get Trekking!"

"Check!"

"What's going on?" asked Garganette, as she watched the panic spreading from mouthpiece to mouthpiece until all the phones were quivering in dread. "When's the party?"

"Party? What party?"

"Er, strictly no party, Gargie babe. See ya, akay? Keep in touch!"

There was one last click and a tender burring filled the air. And then there was peace.

Garganette sat in the silence and thought. It seemed to her that there was nothing for it but for her to visit the Yuppies on their home ground and there and then decided to go to the place where all the people live in freedom, Batcherland.

On The Way To Batcherland

Garganette took her Wimps and her Wimmin, together with those Blacks and Yooves who had joined her, on this journey to Batcherland, because she felt sure that they would enjoy the chance to see for themselves what life was like there: opportunities for travel and mind-broadening among the native peoples of other lands should not be denied, she believed. And besides they whined and cut up rough at the thought of being left behind; so it was a large and gay party that set out on this new adventure. Garganette was much excited: she looked forward very hopefully to seeing this fabled land for herself; she was particularly interested in visiting Torytown, the capital city, not just of Batcherland but also, she had been brought up to believe, of the known free world. She hoped that in Torytown she would at last meet some Yuppies and longed especially to make the acquaintance of the Leader of that place, the Hugely Revered and Respected Mrs Batcher, who was known by some as Batcher the Bold, Brave and Beautiful, or Margaret the Magnificent, while others unaccountably styled her Hilda the Horrible, but to Garganette she was Pegotty the Perplexing.

They had not gone far on the journey when Garganette's sublime reveries were interrupted as the distant sounds of scuffles reached her, coming from somewhere around her ankles, and looking down she saw with dismay that all her party was in turmoil. The Wimmin were accusing each other of unspeakable jealousies, intrigues and faithless lusts, while only joining forces to revile the male members of the party for being wimpish, macho, insensitive, babyish, narrow-minded, bloody-minded and worst of all, generally male; all the Blacks and the Yooves were indulging in hideous racist, sexist, ageist and heightist tensions, and the whole thing was in process of erupting into a general and wholehearted violence, and fists, feet and blood were flying in wild abandonment.

"Whatever is going on here?" cried Garganette, in some

surprise.

A dreadful babble rose up, which because she couldn't understand a word of it, she stopped her ears with her hands and begged they would be quiet.

"Who wants to fight?" she cried.

"Me! Me! Me!" they answered gladly.

"Who doesn't want to fight?"

"Me, please, Garganette," said Claude, shyly, coming out from a large hollow tree, followed by the other Wimps nodding.

"What's the fight about?"

"Me! Me! Me!" cried the Wimmin ecstatically, hugging each other.

"Now, if you're sure you want to fight..."

"Yes!!!" cried all the deadly foes.

"H'm," thought Garganette for a moment. "Well," she said, "I suppose you'd better take up your positions in this conveniently large and open quarry. It must be a clean fight. No weapons except fists, feet, teeth and claws. And please observe the Queensberry guidelines, set down to protect the more delicate regions below the belt. Now, on the given signal you will all engage."

The Wimmin cheered as the combatants rushed to their places with cries of delight. A large crowd gathered around at the edges of the battlefield; Claude prepared to give the signal and just then a thin blue line appeared at Garganette's right instep.

"Allo, allo, allo. What's all this then? Do you require any assistance, Miss?"

"Ah, Officer," said Garganette, ever courteous, "you have arrived in good time to help in ensuring that the crowd doesn't get in the way or get hurt."

"But, Your Hugeness, we can't allow this to go on. My men are here to stop this bloody war!"

"I don't see how that is to be done," said Garganette. "I've thought the whole thing over very carefully. They all want to fight."

"Now, don't you worry your pretty massive head about that, Miss," said the Officer in Charge. "My men will gladly sort it out for you. We'll rush in there and, er, part the persons concerned. We are the Force, after all. And when we've apprehended them all we'll just lock them up for a bit, so they can cool down."

"But we must get to Batcherland this afternoon; we're invited for tea. No, no, Officer, this time your men must protect the crowd, save them from pick-pockets and other sly opportunistic wolves. For the battle and the troops I take full responsibility."

"Ohwoooo!" went the thin blue line in disappointed chorus. "That's not fair!"

"Shall I wave the flag, please Garganette?" asked Claude shyly.

"I think you'd better, Claude," replied Garganette. And a great shout went up as she cried, "Let battle commence!"

What a terrific battle that was! Legs were broken, skulls cracked, limbs torn off, blood and sweat poured in rivers across the quarry until the stones underfoot were slippery with it. Bodies were hurled from one end of the battlesite to the other, whence some bounced back to rejoin the fray, while others lay perfectly still, perhaps to study the sky awhile, perhaps not. One Yoof was split in two, from here to here, I swear it, lost almost all his blood and half his guts along with his liver and lites, but such was the courage displayed that, after taking a moment to recover his wind, he gathered all the bits he could find, stuffed them back in, stitched himself up and with scarcely a groan was ready and willing to fight again. And one of the Blacks, having lost a leg, an arm, two ears and his nose and almost all the rest of his toes, refused to be beaten but with tremendous valour, hopped and leapt about, tripping up any of the enemy who came within reach and then beating them with his own disconnected arm! Amazing!

Blacks fought with Blacks; Yooves with Yooves; Yooves of both sexes fought ditto Blacks, and ditto ditto the Blacks with the Yooves. There was, it was later noted, absolutely no discrimination on the battlefield. It was glorious!

The Wimmin, having screamed themselves hoarse and so lost their voices, swooned with delight at each new example of valorous proof of the fighters' love of them.

The crowd, picnicking at the edges, quaffed lager in vast quantities and singing profane versions of sacred songs, were vehement in their approval of the spectacle, cheering acts of heroism, and railing against cowardice.

Even Claude found himself moved. He leaped up and down in his excitement, scarcely able to contain himself. Twice he almost ran to join the melee, once he fainted, until at last, muttering something about St Crispin's Day and Agincourt, he raced down into the battle and was at once welcomed by being knocked from here to Kingdom Come, where he was later discovered smiling the happy smile of one who knows and has proved his manliness.

The very Gods themselves woke up from a long and ghastly sleep and came post haste from Mount Olympus to watch this stupendous display of unarmed combat on the field. They complimented Garganette most sincerely upon her skills in Generalship, Marshalling her Forces and Organising. She so captivated her divine visitors, who seemed to have forgotten an old and unsavoury quarrel with her ancestors, that she had 17 offers of marriage from Zeus alone, who even went to the trouble of adopting almost 16 different disguises in an effort to discover what her particular fancy might be, and besides this Heracles, Theseus, Apollo and twenty others whose names she never quite caught, all Gods and Heroes, prostrated themselves before her in the hope that she might smile upon them. She, of course, had to refuse them all for fear, apart from any other considerations, of hurting the feelings of those she rejected and so sparking off another of those interminable Olympian feuds, but she declined with such a sweet and overwhelming grace that, before they departed, they vowed eternal friendship and allegiance with her, assuring her of a place among them any time she chose.

At last the battle was over. All those combatants still standing on one or both feet were declared by popular consent the winners. These then began to weep at the hideous damage they had inflicted upon those others who had so recently been their brothers, and knelt among the bodies of the fallen, vowing, that if only they would please get up and smile again, they the Victors would devote the rest of their lives to the cause of restituting them, the Vanquished. And there was much weeping and wailing and gnashing of teeth, rending of hair, tearing of garments and beating of breasts. Then the Wimmin came down to solemnly look to the wounded.

The crowd dispersed in orderly fashion, a mere 2,000 or so in the custody of the Thin Blue Line for various minor and public order offences, and Garganette, seeing how far advanced the day was, decided to spend the night in the nearby heath land, and having made a nice field hospital for the wounded in her open-work straw bag, settled down to sleep.

It was seen in the morning that few were terminally injured and that the number of actual irrecoverable deaths was so limited as to be more or less uncountable, but despite this cheering news, and the lovely breakfast Garganette so expertly provided for them off the land, the party was inclined to be fractious, as people generally are after an orgy, so she swept them all up into her bag and set off down the eventful road to the right, for Batcherland.

Garganette In Batcherland

At last Garganette and her party arrived in Batcherland, where they were greeted by a very harassed and important person who immediately took charge of everything saying, "Oh dear, oh dear! We were getting very worried about you and all our schedules have been upset and we'll have to re-arrange everything. We were expecting you yesterday for tea and here it is almost breakfast tomorrow. Oh dear! Now come along, say a few words into the mike, smile for your photo opportunity, and just wait while we get the TV cameras back. Or maybe we should just fax ahead to Torytown and get them set up there. Oh dear, what shall I do? Come along, over here. Quickly now, there's a car waiting for you. Oh dear, I don't think you're going to fit in. No one told us you'd be quite that large. Couldn't you sort of squeeze yourself up a bit? You're just not trying, are you? Well, I'm glad you find it so amusing, that's all. You just try and do my job. It's very important to have everything correct, you know!"

"Perhaps," said Garganette, "it might be easier if I walk. How far is it to Torytown and in which direction should I go?"

"Walk! You can't possibly walk! It's just not done! It's miles and miles down that road there; it'll take you days and days. And anyway what about us? We've been told to put you in this car and I intend to do it, too!"

"I quite understand," said Garganette. "Arrange a train for my friends here would you, and I'll meet you all in Torytown. So kind of you, thank you for all your help," and she set out.

Now an extraordinary thing happened: while Garganette arrived in Torytown within 30 minutes as the crow flies and taking it easy, the train took five weeks, due to Points Failure, Signals Failure, Snow on the Line, Drought, the Cup Final, Hooliganism, Sheep on the Line, Industrial Action and Bad Management, with the result that she never did see the rest of her party in Torytown.

What a beautiful place Torytown is. How gorgeously the sun,

set in the blue canopy of heaven, shines casting a golden dazzle on the mighty towering temples erected to the Great God of that place, old Mammon himself, where the people worship him in their millions, daily undergoing the most crushing hardships to reach his altars and perform his mysteries, and in solemn electronic rites work the miracle of turning an endless forest of paper into gold for him, asking in return only that he will feather their distant nests. And the people gladly resign their lives to him, for they find that Mammon looks after his own.

"Ah look," said Garganette, surveying the scene, "monuments built by a free people."

And in amongst the towering office blocks were other temples, vast glossy emporia, bursting with every luxury then known; with here and there strange edifices labelled 'McGovern' and 'Eagle Star' and other weird names, which struck a different note somehow and provided a greater density to the rich tapestry being woven all around her.

Garganette was very impressed by the splendidness of all she saw, but could not stay to marvel for it was morning, at that time when millions of people were thronging the pavements, hurrying to their places of work, while the roads were packed with cars, jammed bumper to bumper, perfectly motionless and evidently engaged in some important act of worship, and it was all so crowded that it was difficult for her to know where to put her feet, until she noticed that the city was dotted with little patches of green, which she took to be parks and she reckoned that if she stepped from one to the next, she could cross to Drowning Street without endangering any of the natives.

So she left the busy high ways, with their exciting din and sparkle, stepped over the splendid shops and hotels, and turning away from the magnificent glittering temples, strode neatly into the first little park. But what was this? She could scarcely believe it! A squalid litter of old newspapers and cardboard boxes left out on the grass.

"Well," she said decisively, "the people are so busy at their worship they've obviously forgotten to tidy up this little patch of green and as it will be no problem for me, I will clean it for them," and she bent down, happy to do any little thing for her kind hosts, and began to gather up the debris.

But imagine her surprise to find that packed in the boxes, wrapped in the papers, were people!

"Oh!" she cried, startled.

"Oh!" they cried, coming awake.

"What is this? Is it some experiment or ritual? Is it an endurance test, or protest or game?" she asked.

"What do you mean?" they said. "We live here."

"In boxes? Why? Please explain to me, for I am a stranger here, why do you choose to live this way? I thought everyone here was free."

"Oh well," they said. "Oh yes," they said. "We're free, alright. Everyone's free. It's like this: them with money are free to spend it on food and homes and clothes and travel and pleasure and all those things, and us without money are free to live in cardboard boxes, and starve and do anything else we like that doesn't require money, see? I mean, the streets are paved with gold, aren't they, and we're free to scrape up as much as we can find. See? It's our choice, isn't it? We're freely exercising our freedom of choice, aren't we? See?"

"I see," said Garganette, much puzzled and perplexed.

"You're on your way to see Mrs Batcher, aren't you? Well, you just tell her from us that we think freedom is a great thing."

"Oh, so do I," said Garganette.

"And so what if we go hungry or get cold or ill? So what's a bit of terminal discomfort? Freedom's a great thing. You tell her to come down here and we'll give her the Freedom of Cardboard City! You tell her that see?" then they all began to laugh, and begged her for the price of a cup of tea, and laughed even more when she said she had no Batchergeld, and Garganette marvelled at the spirit of these people who valued their freedom so, they would face death from hunger or cold. Though, however much she puzzled over the question, she couldn't understand why they should find it necessary to exercise their freedom in such a very uncomfortable way. Something, she felt as she continued her way, didn't quite add up, something she couldn't quite put her finger on, made her uneasy, but she was sure that Mrs Batcher would explain everything to her.

'H'mm,' she thought. 'All that talk about starving has made me very hungry. I do hope that Mrs Batcher will have a nice hot breakfast for me.'

Then she stepped delicately among some lions, washed her face at a little fountain, cleaned up Nelson's hat for him and was ready to present herself.

But what was this? The top of Drowning Street was barricaded off, presumably to prevent a large gathering of protesters from charging down the street to No. 10. She bent down for a closer look at them. "Yuppies!" she cried joyfully, recognising them at once. "Real live Yuppies at last! I'm so pleased to meet you."

"Oh, Garganette, you must help us! It's terrible! It's not fair! Interest rates have gone up again, and it's dearer to buy and cheaper to sell and we're losing money," and they knelt as they whispered the sacred word. "Yes actually losing money! It's grossly unfair! You must tell Mrs Batcher that out here on the streets are Estate Agents who can't get the asking price! Yes! And we're driving Skodas," here several paled, "or even travelling by tube! I even lost my in-car personal audio communicator," cried one breaking down altogether, "and we're cooking for ourselves! Spaghetti, yah!"

"Mmm, lovely!" said Garganette.

"It's not lovely! It's shocking! What's happening to the Batcher Miracle? What's happening to US?! Oh, Garganette, please help! You're our last chance," and they clung to her shoe straps pleading until she agreed, willingly enough, to ask Mrs Batcher

138

what the answer was, for she was puzzled by their problems and wished to know what it all meant.

Then she stepped over the barriers, smiled graciously upon the Thin Blue Line who waved back, and, just to make sure there was nothing else in the way, looked around her: first to the right, but she saw nothing much there; then to the left, where she spotted a man in an extremely bright blue suit getting nearer all the time, but there were no further obstacles in her path and she went up to the door of No 10.

Garganette Meets Mrs Batcher

"Ah, Garganette," said Mrs Batcher, who was wearing a nice blue dress with lovely green spots and blotches on it. "Welcome, my dear young woman. You must be hungry after your long journey. Do have some breakfast."

Now, Garganette, while delighted by the breakfast, was puzzled as to how to proceed with Mrs Batcher, for she seemed something very like a tiger disguising itself as a doe, but judging by the width of the shoulder pads and the voice, Garganette finally decided that Mrs Batcher must be one of the Wimmin, and the better to understand her, politely said:

"How do you do, Mrs Batcher. It's so kind of you to meet me. I left several of my people at the border, among whom are some Wimmin with whom I am sure you would have many interests in common. They are particularly anxious that you should help them in their fight for Liberty, Equality and Sisterhood."

"Ah yes. How fascinating. So you still have Wimmin in your country? Here in Batcherland we have no need of such things. We have found it a great satisfaction that everyone here is valued for what they are, and I am glad that I have personally played a small part in that.

"You see, dear," she went on, "you must let me explain it all to you. We have here in Batcherland a society based on the

Individual. We believe the individual to be supremely important, for of course, however many millions there are in a society those millions are made up of individual men and women, and we must never forget this. We believe that everyone must be allowed the freedom to reach his full potential, and have full Freedom of Choice."

"That's wonderful," said Garganette enthusiastically.

"Please let me finish. And so Individual Freedom is the great ideal to which we strive, and we know, we have proven, that by virtue of Hard Work, Thrift, Honest Toil, Education, Industry, the Rule of Law, and by Upholding the Family Way of Life and the Work Ethic, each individual can find his way to maximize his full potential, even to reaching the very highest positions of power. And of course this makes people very happy."

Now this reminded Garganette of the people she had met earlier and she said, "Oh, but Mrs Batcher, there are some Yuppies outside protesting about Interest Rates and in the Park..."

"Ah yes, the dear little Yuppies are learning some very valuable lessons about Market Forces and allowing the Market to find its own Level. It's all part of their education, for which come to think of it, we should be charging them at the Market Rate. H'm."

"And also, Mrs Batcher, what about the poor people?"

"Poor people?" said Mrs B.

"Yes, I found some, in a park, living in cardboard boxes."

"It's extraordinary I agree. We find it most remarkable. They've been given every advantage: a State Education and Family Income Support and all this Freedom, and what do they do with it? Living in cardboard boxes! But we can't force them to live in houses. They've chosen their beds and must lie in them."

"Yes but even so, what if they've made a wrong choice?" said Garganette.

"What!" cried Mrs Batcher, who had never made a wrong choice and didn't know it was possible. "My dear young woman,

140

you really must try to understand that by following the rules, by working hard and always being right, you can become whatever you are most fit for. Why, look at me! I was born of honest humble shopkeepers and now look where I am. We've even become a Grandmother! Have you ever been a Grandmother? No? But you will, you must. It is the most wonderful experience to see your own child holding his child. In fact ever since this happened to us, we feel that we can go on and on!"

"But," Garganette began.

"Please let us finish what we were saying. And on and on. Oh, it's so invigorating! How very good of you to call! Do drop in again sometime for another lesson. Now we really must be off: we have a very busy day ahead of us in the House, Roasting Kinnock; Dressing down the Salads; to say nothing of Boiling up the Greens! You must come over to dinner one day, we have enjoyed our chat! Goodbye! Goodbye!" and suddenly Garganette found herself in the street again, while Mrs Batcher rode away in a silver haze on a golden cloud.

'Goodness,' thought Garganette, her head in a bit of a whirl, and she almost tripped over someone.

How Garganette Meets A Juggler

"Oh I'm so sorry," she said, fearful she might have hurt him, and bending down, recognised the man in the bright blue suit whom she'd noticed earlier making his slow progress towards Drowning Street. But as she looked she saw that the suit was not entirely blue, but was red and green also, with splashes of yellow and orange, and then she realised who it was.

"Why Mr Pinnock," she cried. "How lovely to meet you."

"Oh it's you Garganette is it? Where did you spring from? You've made me drop everything, look you."

"Oh I'm sorry. Let me help you pick them up. But what do you want all these things for?" she asked as she handed him various odd articles.

"I'm a juggler, aren't I girl, and I have to keep all this up in the air, or people lose faith in me, isn't it."

"But what is it you're juggling with? I've never seen things like this before."

"Statistics, of course! Look I'll show you. Stand back a bit, girl. That's right. Here we go. There's Unemployment, Inflation, Women, Blacks..."

"Women as statistics?" she asked.

"Well of course, look you. We have to get all the figures before we can give women true equality, redress the imbalances."

"What imbalances?" asked Garganette.

"Er. Yes. Well, never mind that now. I'll explain it later. Then there's the Balance of Payments, Interest Rates, Mortgages, the Health Service and Crippling Strikes. Homelessness, Taxes for the Rich, Private Education and the National Curriculum. Now we just add the Dream of a Rosy Future masked in a Haze of Confidence. Then a hefty weight of Anti-Batcherism, a lot of irony and tired contempt and, wait for it, here's the big one of the moment, dadah THE POLL TAX, my ace. So what do you think of that?"

"My goodness," said Garganette watching him juggling his

statistics so skillfully, "I've never seen such balls!"

"Oh that's nothing!" he cried enthusiastically."That's just to show you what I mean. You should see me when I really get going."

"But what does it mean?" said Garganette. "What do you do it for?"

"Why to win the election, of course. Oh really Garganette, you're so naive!"

"But Mr Pinnock, I thought politics was to do with listening to the people. Something about a sacred trust to carry out their will?"

"Ha ha ha. O ho ho ho! Oh sorry Garganette. Listen it's important you realise that this is not opportunism, but a serious question of having principles that appeal to everybody, evoke their responses, fulfil their expectations, play up to all kinds of foolishnesses in order to liberate them from their prejudices, and all in all to satisfy the Law of Statistical Convictions."

"Well," said Garganette, "I never knew that!"

"Oh you're a good girl, Garganette. I'm only too happy to have cleared up any little doubts or confusions you may have had. You know, you'd be very useful to us in the party, look you. Just leave your name and address and we'll send you the form. Well, I must rush now as I've very important business to attend to, baiting Mrs Batcher in the House. So long now, Garganette, bye-bye. Cheerio," and he rushed away juggling with all his might.

How Garganette Meets
Another Very Important Person

Garganette watched the colourful clown as he raced away, and turning to leave Drowning Street saw a large car pulling up, out of which several stern broad-shouldered men emerged with, in their midst, a most charming gentleman who smiled confidently upon all he saw. He kissed the journalists and television crews, he kissed the policemen, the politicians and a passing postman. "Mr Borbachov, as I live and breathe!" exclaimed Garganette. "I'm so pleased to meet you, as there is much I would like to discuss with you."

"Ah Garganette. I too am delighted to meet you. I have heard you are the champion of freedom in your own way, just as I work towards the great goal of liberation for my people. I'm sure there is much you could learn from me, if you heed my advice and follow my example. For too long my people have been oppressed by the dead hand of corruption and by their inability to grasp freedom. They have apathetically allowed wolves disguised as shepherds to fleece them of the product of their labour. Now they must learn to resist this tyranny, to stand up as men, learn to be free. And it's so simple, you see. Ha ha! Already they speak and argue, openly publish dissent, make intelligent questions where for so long they have bowed the head, scarcely daring to dream opposition. Now they begin to stand upright for I am at the front, braving the snarl of the wolves. I am not afraid. I will lead my people and they will be free!"

"Oh, Mr Borbachov, that's so exciting. And then what will you do?"

"My dear young woman, I do not understand you."

"Well, you came to power, uninvited by your people, as a tyrant, and until they are free you remain a tyrant. But when the liberation comes they won't need a tyrant any more. What will you do then?"

"No, no, Garganette, they will always need me for as long as I have breath in my body to lead them. I'm afraid there is yet much you don't understand. The people must have a tyrant to lead them, and they are very lucky to have me, for I insist that they be free. Others have not been so kind!"

"I see," said Garganette, in some confusion. "You mean your people are so used to tyranny that they need a tyrant to teach them how to be free?"

"That's it exactly. I'm glad you understand. They could never do it by themselves."

"I'm sure you're right," said Garganette, "but I always had a different idea of freedom."

"Ah," said Mr Borbachov, wisely. "You English have strange notions: dreaming here on your island you have little idea of what the real world is like. Well, it has been a great pleasure to teach you, but I must go now. Goodbye."

"Thank you for this lesson in freedom," said Garganette, "but there is still one thing I'm interested to hear your views on."

"You do have an enquiring mind. Well, well, I can give you a few more moments, so ask me, child, and I will tell you."

"People grasping at freedom react in different ways, I've noticed, and if they are not clear of their goals the consequences of sudden liberation can be strange. They forget what they were striving for, there is confusion and violence erupts, blood is spilt, innocent people suffer, but I'm sure you know the kind of thing I mean."

"Oh really Garganette! You exasperate me. Your questions are puerile. Well, well, I must not be hard on you for you are still a child. Perhaps when I have more time, I will be able to give you more instruction, but now I have matters of world importance to discuss with the Leader of this great land. Remember this: I will lead the people and they *will* be free! Goodbye!"

How Garganette Leaves Batcherland
In Search Of Truth

The speed with which events followed one on the other in Batcherland left Garganette almost breathless, and feeling that there was still much for her to learn, she left that country. It was a fine autumn day and she wandered alone and robustly loitering on the way, musing on all she had seen and encountered. Just this side of the border she lay down on the grass covered land to feel the warmth of it around her, and she reflected peacefully on how like the earth she was herself: warm, solid, large, contented, her own hills and valleys, and outcroppings mirrored in her surroundings. And she felt a heartbeat rhythm and listening closely couldn't quite tell if it was her own or not. Her head lolled deeper, her body spread itself, her eyes drifted closed, but just before she fell asleep, just before she toppled into the pit of oblivion, just as she was about to slip gratefully into the arms of old seductive Morpheus for blissful consummation, her attention was caught by a tiny sound, which decided her not to sleep but to be wakeful and see what would happen next. And there it was: a green little man, very pretty, with big soft brown eyes and a big soft red mouth. Their eyes met and he started like a young roe deer caught unawares whilst feeding.

"Oh," he said, eyes staring wide in confusion."I didn't see you there!"

"How come?" said Garganette. "I'm big enough."

"You seemed so much a part of the land you're lying in. As I approached, I thought you were a particularly lovely mound or hill, or series of hills. You see, I'm a Green and I thought you were a Site of Special Interest, as we call them, and I was going to check you out and stick a preservation order on you."

"Mmm," said Garganette, stretching langorously. "Sit down and tell me all about it."

"Thank you, yes. Well, you know, we Greens care deeply about the Earth. You see, for centuries Man has just raped and

146

plundered and taken what he wants without putting anything back and without caring what happens in the future. But the future is now and getting shorter all the time. I mean, the shameful way industry uses all the fossil fuels, digging huge craters, tearing out the coal, burning down the forests for agriculture, creating deserts where once were beautiful eco-systems, poisoning the seas so that the fishes and mammals die of horrible diseases, torturing poor beasts for their meat, hens for their eggs - Oh, it's too much!" and he began to weep.

"There, there," said Garganette, patting him gently to comfort him and almost weeping herself in sympathy.

"You see how awful it is?" he cried. "And it's almost too late! But there's still time, there's just still time enough to avert a major catastrophe. If we stop pouring chemicals into the atmosphere, stop using nuclear energy, stop burning forests and fossil fuels. Stop poisoning the Earth. If we free the animals, use alternative sources of energy, like wind power or the sun, and begin to live in harmony with Nature instead of trying always to dominate; begin to care for and tend the Earth, our lovely Mother Earth, to hold her in our arms and nurture her with gratitude for all the goodness she so generously provides us with. Ooooh!" and he was forced once again by tears to stop, for he was so moved by the picture he saw of a beautiful, loving Earth locked in a beautiful mutual embrace with all her children, human and otherwise, living in a divine Earthly Paradise.

"You see," he went on in his sweet gentle voice, while his eyes, almost dry again, shone with his prophetic vision. "You see how beautiful everything could be, will be? And when I came along just now, not realising it was you," he blushed a little, "I thought you the most beautiful landscape I had ever seen and I wanted very much to explore you."

"And so you shall," said Garganette, quite won over to his cause, for he was very soft and pretty, all in his green. "I live here in me, and I can show you all the best places to explore. You can get to know the earth. Come here, I'll show you where to swim.

Come here, my little fish," and she brought him tenderly to her.

"O! Oh dear," he said and he began to whimper.

"Now what's the matter, sweetling? Come closer, little one. Here, just here, that's the way. Take off your little shirt and now your trousers, dear, for it's better to swim naked."

"Oh oh oh," he cried in some distress, screwing up his eyes and clinging to her finger.

"Why whatever can it be? Don't you want to swim with me?"

"Yes. O! I mean I think so."

"Well what is it that makes you hesitate? Tell me, little mackerel, tell me do."

"But I can't! I can't swim!"

"Well, never mind. I'll teach you, it's so easy and so nice. The nicest way of being close to Mother Nature that I know."

"Oh, not today! Please not today," and he begged so imploringly that Garganette kissed him, which while softening his resistance, stiffened his resolve, so that, under her excellent tuition, he soon learnt to swim and so well that it was as if he had spent his entire life doing nothing else.

Later while they were drying themselves off, he suddenly threw his arms passionately around her wrist saying:

"O Garganette, my own true love, you must marry me!"

"What?" cried Garganette, who thought she must have misheard.

"Yes, my dear love, my own, you shall be mine. We shall build a beautiful house in some quiet, unspoiled corner of the land and have dozens of children, as many as you like, and I shall protect you!"

"H'mm," said Garganette, "and what would we do for money, my dear?"

"Money! Ha!" he said scornfully. "Who cares for that!"

"Well," she said, "if you are to build a house and have all those children, money will be necessary."

"I see," he said. "H'm. Very well. I shall get the money from my cousin, who is doing very well in the plastics industry. He will

148

give me the cash I need."

"Give it to you?" said Garganette, surprised. "Why should he do that? And anyway whoever I marry must work for his living."

"Then I shall take up his offer of a job and work with him in his company," said the little Green, decisively. "Naturally, I shall have to start at the bottom, but I shall soon work my way up and I am sure that before long I shall have proved myself worthy of the partnership which is anyway my due."

"Work with him in plastics?" said Garganette, amazed. "What about the pollution?"

"How can you think of such matters, Garganette, when I have my children to worry about? But where are my clothes?" and he began hurriedly to dress.

"You know, I'm not entirely sure," said Garganette gently, "that you and I would be ideally suited as marriage partners."

"But why not?" he cried as he tied his shoelaces.

"Oooo, just a feeling I have," she said.

"You women are such funny superstitious creatures with your feelings," he said, patting her toes lightly.

"But I shouldn't worry," she added, "there are hundreds of other fish you can swim with."

"Oh that," he said and tittering, blushed. "I don't know. But if you're sure, about us marrying?"

"Quite sure," she said.

"Then I can only thank you, Garganette, for giving me my freedom. But where is my briefcase?" he said in a panic.

"You haven't got one," she said.

"Not got one!" he cried. "I shall have to buy one. And a calculator, and a personal computer, and a car phone. And a car! Good bye, dear Garganette! Goodbye!" and he dashed away in his dark blue suit.

"Come back," cried Garganette and caught him by his coat tails. "Where are you going?"

"I've got to catch the 7.48 to town!" he cried, struggling to get free.

"And work in plastics?" said Garganette. "What about Mother Earth?"

"Oh!" he cried.

"You can't just give up all that you've believed in," she said. "Have you thought of being a small farmer? You could marry a nice girl and live off the land. Think, you could care for the Earth and the animals in a good and loving way."

"Oh, but Garganette," he whined, "it's such hard work and so dull!"

"Ha ha!" she laughed. "Well, I suppose it depends on what you're used to. In that case, why not go to the city and find other people like yourself, who care for this earth? You could work with them to bring about a change. Think of your children and their future. And you're very well placed, as your cousin may be willing to listen to your arguments. You might not get rich but you wouldn't be bored. And don't forget how fashionable green is right now."

"Yes, that's true. And it's a Just Cause. You're so clever Garganette," said the dear little Green, happy again, and they parted the best of friends.

How Garganette Makes A Decision

Garganette stood up and reached for the sky. She had great issues on her mind and for a moment she idly pushed the clouds around in deep abstraction. A great shout from over to the East caught her attention and she looked to see millions of people across half a continent cheering in celebration at their great festival of freedom. Over to the west the sun blazed, getting low on the horizon and she stood alone in a garden land.

Now, it may seem strange to the gentle reader, but it is nevertheless the absolute truth that sweet Garganette had not till this day considered marriage, when the little Green had suggested it to her, and that was odd, for all young women dream of

150

marriage, don't they? But the problem was, who should she, Garganette, young Giantess of the World, who could she, assuming that she should want to, who on Earth could she marry? Then it was that she came to her decision.

She took pen and paper and wrote the following letter:

Dear Mr Porgie,

I am going across the seven seas to roam the seven continents, like my father before me. But the treasure I seek is not gold or precious jewels. I look for other Giants like myself, for a giant like me needs a giant man to love. A man with a big you-know, certainly, but not just that. I want a man with a big heart and a vast mind. And when I find them, I shall bring them back to you, for only you, dear Mr Porgie, can say who is truly a Giant.

With all my love from

Garganette x x x x x x x

Then she put it in an envelope with a first class stamp, addressed it to :

> Mr G Porgie
> First Class Male

sealed it with a kiss, popped it in the letter box, and with a light heart and much expectant excitement, she set out, over the sea and away.

POSTSCRIPT

Well, what do you think of that, then?

What? What do you mean is that all? Isn't that enough? I've been hours at this, hours and hours. Days even. Look, my fingers are weak with exhaustion from all that writing. My brow is fevered with thought. Mop my fevered brow for me, my love. How do I look? Am I pale and interesting? Oh, my heart is beating strangely! You say the most wonderful things!

Oh, I see. You want to know what happens next. You feel there are questions left unanswered. You want me to tell you where Garganette's search took her? What wondrous adventures she had? Did she find Giantland, or only fools and charlatans masquerading in big boots, and how could she tell which was which? Did she wander the pretty globe she calls home on a fruitless, though entertaining, journey, or did she find that one giant whom she could love for his special qualities? And where did she find him? And was he a poet or a philosopher? Or what?

Well, it's very interesting that you should ask, and I've got all the answers to your very intelligent questions right here in my noddle, safe in my memory bag, just as my mother told me, and you know who she learned it from. And later on I might tell you what happened to sweet Garganette, or I might not, but right now we're going to celebrate this glorious life with music and wine, good food, good fellowship and love, and hurray! here are our friends at the door.